Books by Helen Van Slyke
available from New English Library:

THE HEART LISTENS
THE MIXED BLESSING
THE BEST PLACE TO BE
ALWAYS IS NOT FOREVER
THE RICH AND THE RIGHTEOUS
THE BEST PEOPLE

THE SANTA ANA WIND

Helen Van Slyke
Writing as Sharon Ashton

NEW ENGLISH LIBRARY

All of the characters in this book are fictitious, and any resemblance to actual persons, living or dead, is purely coincidental.

First published in the USA in 1974 by Doubleday & Company, Inc.

First published in Great Britain in 1975 by New English Library

First NEL Paperback Edition January 1982

NEL Books are published by
New English Library,
Barnard's Inn, Holborn,
London EC1N 2JR, a division of Hodder and Stoughton Ltd.

Typeset by Rabcroft
Printed and bound in Great Britain by
Cox & Wyman Ltd, Reading

0 450 05283 4

For Clinton Halsey

THE SANTA ANA WIND

Chapter One

THE TALL, black Spanish iron gates swung open and a young Mexican boy touched his hat respectfully as the big station wagon slid smoothly through. The two hulking men who flanked me in the front seat nodded at the boy who closed the portals behind us with a decisive, resounding clash. The sound seemed to have an ominous air of finality, as though we had entered some foreign fortress sealed off from the inquisitive eyes of the outside world. For a moment I had a terrible understanding of how it must feel to go to prison, to be confined behind a high stone wall like the one that surrounded this vast, silent estate.

It was ridiculous, of course. I was not entering a fortress or a jail. On the contrary, I was a twenty-four-year-old bride entering my new home, the Trippe estate in Southern California, not twenty-five miles from downtown Los Angeles. My companions were not captors or jailers. On my right was my new husband and on my left his brother who had come to meet us at the airport not more than an hour before. I had been married only that morning to Dr. Roger Trippe, a man I deeply loved, though in a way he was almost a stranger to me. Roger and I had met in the Children's Hospital in Washington, D.C., where I was a nurse and he was completing his pediatric residency. It had been a rapid courtship and a quick marriage because he was eager to return to his native California and go into practice with two other pediatricians – his brother André and a close friend Dr. Wilson Wiseman.

In the brief three months that Roger and I had known each other, he had told me of this extraordinary place where he had grown up.

'You'll love Madrugada,' he'd said. 'It's the Spanish word for "Daybreak." And well named. We have sunrises out there, sweetheart, like you Easterners have never seen. There are seven hundred acres, mostly woods, with trees that were centuries old before the first Spaniards got to California. My family has lived there for four generations. My great-grandfather probably bought it for ten cents an acre or something ridiculous like that. Over the years, it's become a modern compound. Each of us has his own house, but we share a communal swimming pool and a tennis court. Of course, our pride is the stables. You'll learn to ride, darling. Josh Jenkins is in charge of the horses and he taught us all. He'll teach you. You'll be an equestrian like the rest of the family – André, Dolores, Drew, all of us.'

It sounded like a dream come true. Not only the

luxurious land but Roger's easy mention of his family, his ties going back hundreds of years.

I had no such ties. At the age of one month I'd been adopted by Sam and Mildred Barlow, a dear, loving, middle-class couple who had given me a good childhood, a normal, happy upbringing in a modest but comfortable home in Maryland. No little girl could have hoped for more love and tenderness than I received from these wonderful people who loved me as though I was the child they were unable to have. I adored my adoptive parents and, when I was old enough to understand, I was also grateful to them for taking into their home and their hearts a baby whose own mother had given her away. And yet, from the day, at the age of seven, I'd learned that Sam and Mildred Barlow were not my real parents I had yearned to know my true identity. It was a need that had begun early and had stayed with me to this day. Mother and Dad, as I thought of the Barlows, could shed no light on my background. They had applied for a baby through a reputable adoption agency in Washington, and I was the result of that application. They were told only that I came of a good background and that the mother had requested that I be named Virginia. The records of my birth were, by law, sealed. I was simply Virginia, a baby with no heritage except a tiny ring, a child's ring, which an unknown mother had left for me. Sam and Mildred gave me the ring when I was seven. It did not even fit over the tip of my little finger, but I wore it always on a gold chain around my neck, my only link with the woman who had borne me. I could feel it now, under my dress, a miniature circle set with six vari-colored stones.

For the thousandth time I wondered about my real parents. Did they love each other and me? Did I come from good, healthy stock? Or was there – most terrible thought – some hereditary illness or madness that I could pass on to children of my own? Was I illegitimate? Was my mother some woman I might pass on a street in Washington? Did I have brothers and sisters? It was terrible to have no history, no knowledge of those who had come before me. Yet it was a most natural curiosity, one that I knew was shared by thousands of other adopted children.

I don't mean to sound as though this curiosity was the obsession of my life, but I'm sure that the helplessness of children led me into pediatric nursing. I identified with them and wanted to make them well and happy. Undoubtedly this same interest in children accelerated my falling in love with Roger who had chose to specialize in their care. I couldn't wait to see the clinic that he, André and Wilson Wiseman operated. I even hoped they would let me work with them, at least until Roger and I started a family of our own. That was my greatest desire: to have children who would be secure and certain of their identities.

We had been driving for some minutes up a narrow, tree-lined road. So far I had seen nothing of the houses or stables that Roger had described. Only a thickly shaded, curving driveway which seemed to lead nowhere. The three of us had talked almost easily on the freeway from Los Angeles here, though Roger did most of the questioning while André gave polite but somewhat restrained answers to my husband's inquiries about their parents, about André's wife, Dolores, and his son, Drew, about the clinic and Wil Wiseman. Now we were silent. Had been since we came through the gates. I knew that our first stop would be at the 'main house' where Roger's parents lived. The men seemed almost to be bracing themselves for this call on 'the Señor and the Señora' as they referred to them. The farther into the compound we drove, the more tense they became. There was something strange, like fear or dread, in the atmosphere, strong enough to make me tremble. My right hand which lay in the hand of my new husband seemed like a fluttering bird at the end of my arm. Roger squeezed my fingers gently.

'Don't be nervous,' he said. 'The Trippe family en masse will adore you. You might not be able to tell it from old dour-face there, but I can tell you've already captivated André.'

I fingered my diamond wedding band nervously as I looked at André. His face held a half-sardonic smile. He doesn't like me, I thought suddenly. He isn't happy about this marriage. For some reason I couldn't fathom, he resented my presence and, with chilling certainty, I felt that my brother-in-law's thinly veiled displeasure represented the attitude of the whole family. For a moment I was tempted to ask him why, but before I could succumb to the impulse André turned the car into a semi-circular drive in front of the ugliest house I'd ever seen. It was a house like those pictured on the covers of books about English mansions on the moors, a huge stone castle, all gray, with chimneys and turrets, a dark, forbidding three-story house that seemed to have no place in the casual climate of California. My bewilderment and dismay must have shown clearly on my face, because Roger hastened to reassure me.

'You're right,' he said. 'It's a monstrosity. But don't worry, Ginny, you won't have to spend much time in it. We have own own house, remember? Each of the other three are quite different than this mausoleum, I promise you.'

'The other *three*?' I repeated. 'I thought there were only two other houses, ours and André's.'

André gave Roger a look that was half-accusatory, half-amused. My husband's face flushed.

'The third house is for our sister, Lila,' he said. 'She lives there with a nurse-companion called Miss Miles.'

I was astonished. In these months of telling me about his family – his parents, Simon and Natalie, André and Dolores and their adopted twenty-year-old son, Drew – Roger had never once mentioned the existence of a sister. Why had he deliberately avoided telling me about her? And why did she have to have a nurse-companion? I was about to ask when André opened the car door on the driver's side.

'Come along,' he said, 'we can't sit here all day. The venerable parents will wonder what we're talking about, and God knows we don't want the Señor to be any more irritable than he normally is.'

Roger helped me out of the station wagon. The sight of the massive front door filled me again with a sense of foreboding that increased when it was opened by an enormous, unsmiling, white-haired woman dressed in black. Her vast bulk filled the doorway and her expression held no welcome. My relief when Roger greeted her was overwhelming.

'Well, there's my glamour girl!' he said. 'How are you Mrs. Angus?'

'Very well, thank you, Mr. Roger.'

'Good. Darling, this is Mrs. Angus who keeps house for my parents. Mrs. Angus, my wife, Virginia.'

I held out my hand. 'I'm so happy to meet you,' I said. It was true. For a terrible moment I'd thought that this was Natalie Trippe, my mother-in-law. Now, looking at her more closely, I realized that she could not be André and Roger's mother. In spite of the white hair and the severe dress, her face, bare of make-up, was only lightly lined, and the sharp blue eyes, despite their coldness, were not those of an elderly woman. She couldn't be more than fifty, I thought. Perhaps even less. And André, I knew, was forty-five.

Mrs. Angus touched my hand briefly, almost reluctantly.

'Best wishes,' she said.

'Thank you.' Once again I sensed the same lack of warmth I had felt in André's attitude, and a fresh wave of uncertainty swept over me. If Mrs. Angus, who lived with the senior Trippes, was displeased by my presence, certainly that displeasure reflected the feelings of her employers. I tried to tell myself that this recurring feeling of rejection was nonsense. I was nervous and my imagination was getting the better of me. It was only because everything was so strange – this gigantic estate that seemed like a foreign country, André's aloofness, Roger's unexpected revelation of a sister and now this cold reception at the door of his parents' home. It added up to nothing tangible, and yet I felt threatened and alone and very far from home.

Roger, his arm around me protectively, led me into the big house and down a long hallway covered with dim portraits in heavy, baroque frames. André and Mrs. Angus followed silently. At the door of the main salon, we paused.

'Don't let the old man scare you,' Roger said under his breath. 'He's been playing the fierce patriarch so long it's become part of his image. He barks but seldom bites.'

I nodded and tried to smile as we entered the gloomy, somber drawing room. It was enormous, at least sixty feet long and forty wide. Heavy velvet draperies closed out the late afternoon sun and a few low lamps burned dimly. The furniture was massive and uncomfortable looking, huge carved mahogany sofas and tall, straight-backed chairs set stiffly against the walls. There was only one appealing touch: a delicate, well-painted, full-length portrait of a beautiful, smiling young girl, her face bathed in sunlight, the white collar of her riding shirt open to show the softly tanned tones of her skin. The portrait was hung prominently on the stone chimney wall over the vast fireplace in front of which stood Simon and Natalie Trippe.

As though we were being presented at court, Roger and I stepped forward to greet his parents. My husband shook hands firmly with his father and then bent to kiss the cheek of the silent, pretty woman who stood beside him.

'Mother, Father, this is Virginia.'

There was a pause. Obviously everyone was waiting for Simon to speak. Rudely, he stared at me, taking in every detail of my features, analyzing me, I thought, as dispassionately as he might examine a brood mare he was about to purchase. Don't flinch, I told myself. With all the composure I could summon I gazed back at him, seeing a stocky, muscular man in his seventies. He was much shorter than his two sons, but he looked well able to beat them physically if necessary. There was a cruelness in the almost-black eyes, and strength in the hard, firm-jawed face, deeply lined around those eyes. His mouth was almost covered by a thick, bushy white mustache.

'You're a surprise,' he said.

Startled, I looked at Roger. Certainly I had not

expected an effusive welcome from this domineering little man, but I had hoped for some kind of civilized greeting, no matter how lukewarm. Roger nodded almost imperceptibly. Play along, the nod seemed to say. Don't cross him, no matter how odd he seems.

'A pleasant one, I hope, sir,' I said.

'That remains to be seen, doesn't it?' Simon answered. 'You seemed to be in a great rush to marry my son.'

I turned scarlet with anger at the implication that I had 'trapped' Roger. And my anger was equally directed at my husband who was permitting me to be received as though I were some housemaid who had been hired without parental approval. Damn it, why didn't Roger speak out? Why were they all so terrified of this little tyrant with his unspeakable manners and his insulting inferences? To my relief, Roger intervened.

'The rush was not Virginia's, Father,' he said. 'It was mine. For reasons we all very well understand, don't we?'

For a moment I thought Simon was going to strike the thirty-year-old man who was his younger son. Instead, the black eyes bored into Roger with a look of outrage that seemed to promise punishment. Then Simon turned away, apparently dismissing us. As though on cue, Natalie Trippe moved toward me, a small smile on her face and kindness and compassion in her eyes. She was a tall, slender woman, blonde like her two sons, frail yet remarkably young looking for one who had to be deep into her sixties. In that instant I imagined what a beauty she must have been as a bride. In her youth she must have been as lovely as the girl in the painting. How could she have married this arrogant man and accepted, as she so clearly had, his ruthless, tyrannical behavior for nearly half a century?

'We're happy you're here, Virginia,' Natalie said. 'I'm sorry we couldn't be at your wedding. I hope your mother received my letter.'

'Yes she did,' I answered. 'It's too bad that Mr. Trippe wasn't well enough to travel East.' I looked at her directly. It was obvious that Simon Trippe could have traversed the Colorado Rapids alone if he had chosen. Apparently he did not choose to see his son married, at least not to me. Natalie Trippe knew that I knew that now, but we both pretended otherwise. I liked my mother-in-law, but I sensed that I would never be close to her. Simon would not permit that, and she would never cross him.

'Roger, dear,' she was saying now, 'I'm sure that you and Virginia are anxious to see your own house. And you must be tired from the excitement and the trip. Tomorrow you must tell me all about the wedding.' Natalie turned to me. 'We'll expect you for Sunday dinner, and perhaps then we'll have time to chat.' She hesitated. 'We *are* happy you're here,' she repeated. Then she glanced at her husband who was preoccupied with a book at the far end of the room. 'You mustn't mind if Mr. Trippe seems a bit brusque,' she said in a soft voice. 'He rather fancies arranging things himself. He was disappointed that you and Roger did not have the ceremony at Madrugada. You see, André was married here and Simon hoped the same for Roger. He's only a bit put out, my dear. It's nothing personal, I assure you.'

She was pathetically trying to apologize for her husband's boorish behavior. I didn't believe a word of the story. There was much more to Simon's anger than the location of the wedding. Even Roger's oblique reference to 'reasons we all understand' was evidence of that.

'Thank you,' I said. 'I'm sure I'll be happy here, Mrs. Trippe. Roger and I love each other very much, and that's all that matters, isn't it?'

A shadow of sadness crossed her face. 'Yes, of course,' she said. 'That's all that matters.' Again she looked at the far end of the room. Simon's rigid back was toward us. Quickly Natalie gave me a little kiss on the cheek. It was the first demonstration of warmth I'd felt since my arrival. I could have wept with gratitude.

We left the big house as quietly as we'd entered it. Silently, André began to drive us to our own place. Roger had told me that it was about a mile from his parents' home, but we passed no other houses and finally I asked André where he and Dolores lived.

'All the houses are on different roads,' he said. 'You can't see one from the other. You'll discover them all in time. Ours and Lila's.'

'I'll give you a tour, darling,' Roger said. 'There's also a little pool house and, of course, the stables. But now I'm anxious to get home, aren't you?'

I nodded. 'Very anxious.' I did not add that I was also not a little apprehensive. My view of Madrugada, until now, had been far different than my mental picture of it. What if my own house was as formidable as the one we'd just left? Never mind. I'd change it into the kind of place I wanted – bright, light and cheerful. I knew that Roger would let me do anything I wanted with it. He'd already said so. But as it turned out, there was no need. The car had stopped in front of a honeymoon cottage – a rambling, one-story house painted creamy yellow. Window boxes outside every room spilled a profusion of ivy and geraniums, and the landscaping was perfection, tree-shaded and dotted with clumps of bright-colored flowers, all of it neither too formally ordered not too wild. I caught my breath with delight.

'Like it?' Roger asked.

'Like it! Oh, darling, I love it! It's a dream house! Hurry up and let me out. I can't wait to see the inside!'

I scrambled from the car and ran up the front path, Roger, pleased as a child, right behind me. We didn't even remember to thank André for driving us home. We simply stood, hand in hand, in front of the door, smiling at each other while André unloaded the bags and drove off without another word. I had, for the moment, forgotten everything bewildering and unpleasant that had gone before. I saw only my very first house, the place where I would raise our children in sunshine and clear air and love.

When this door opened there was no giantess in sight. Instead, we were greeted by a pretty young Mexican girl whose face was wreathed in a welcoming smile.

'Señor. Señora. *Buenos días.* I am Rosita.'

I loved her on sight. 'Hello, Rosita. I'm Mrs. Trippe.' The words sounded strange. It was the first time I'd spoken my new name aloud.

The girl continued to smile. 'I know, Señora.'

Roger grinned. 'And you're Carmelita's niece, I know that. Señora Dolores wrote that she had engaged you for us, but I'd have known anyway. You're as pretty as your aunt.'

Rosita blushed. 'I hope you and the Señora will be pleased.'

'I'm sure we will be,' I said. 'Come on, Roger. Let's go in! We're standing on our own doorstep like two idiots!'

As we started to enter the house, the expression on Rosita's face was so pained that I stopped.

'What's wrong? Is something the matter?'

The girl dropped her glance, than shyly looked at Roger. 'Please, Señor, I know it is not my place, but have you not forgotten something?'

Roger looked puzzled. 'Forgotten something? Oh, you mean the bags. We'll get them in a few minutes.'

Rosita shook her head. 'Not the suitcases, Señor. I will bring them. Have you not forgotten the custom? I see many people marry. Always the husband carries his bride for the first time into their house. I think it is very romantic. You do not mind if I say this to you?'

Roger and I exchanged smiles.

'I love you for saying it, Rosita,' I told her.

'And I thank you,' Roger added. 'I'd never have forgiven myself if I'd forgotten to carry the Señora over the threshold. For that matter, she'd probably never have forgiven me either. My dear little Rosita, you probably have saved a marriage!'

Laughing he scooped me up in his big arms and, to Rosita's delight and my own, carried me easily into the hallway of our sparkling, perfect little house. All my uneasiness seemed to disappear. I never had felt so happy. I did not know how quickly my happiness would turn to terror.

Chapter Two

I COULDN'T get over the beauty of the house that was now mine. Knowing it had been Roger's in his bachelor days, I'd expected, at best, a mannish, functional interior which I was prepared to soften into a home for a family. Instead I'd walked, or more accurately, been carried, into a bright, airy, cheerful cottage done in soft woods and white wicker with gay flower prints that picked up the colors of the garden outside.

I ran delightedly through the tastefully furnished rooms, complete down to the last ash tray. The comfortable living room with its deep sofa and inviting chairs adjoined a cozy, book-lined study. Beyond was a small, elegant dining room and a spotless modern kitchen and laundry area. The sleeping quarters on the other side of the house were composed of a big master bedroom, dressing room and bath, a suite feminine enough to please a woman yet not so delicate that a big man like Roger would feel uneasy in it. There was a fair-sized guest room and bath which I immediately visualized as a nursery. In time, as we had children, we would need more space. But that would not be a problem. The house seemed designed for easy additions. It could sprawl gracefully over much more of its five-acre plot.

Roger was pleased with my enthusiasm.

'You amaze me,' I said. 'I had no idea you had decorating as well as doctoring abilities!'

'I'd like to take credit for it,' he said, 'but truthfully I can't. It was pretty much a mess when I left it a couple of years ago. When I knew I was going to bring you here I asked Dolores to see what she could do. I must say she's done wonders in six weeks! Of course, darling, you're free to change it any way you'd like.'

'Right now I don't see how it could be improved,' I said. 'It's beautiful. André's lucky to have a wife with such taste. I can't wait to meet her and thank her.'

'She'll be pleased and relieved that you like it. She was a little reluctant to take on the assignment. Said it was unfair to hand any woman a house decorated by a stranger, and she didn't really know your taste, except for what she gleaned from my glowing descriptions of you in general. I told her to do it the way *she'd* like it. I had a hunch that you two would see eye to eye.'

His obvious affection and admiration for his sister-in-law warmed me. Any woman who had such a sense of rightness must be perceptive as well as kind.

'What's she like?' I asked.

'Dolores?' He seemed to be considering his answer. 'Beautiful. Same age as André – forty-five. They've been married twenty-one, no, twenty-two years, I guess. I remember their wedding. I was the ring-bearer in a horrible little white satin suit. I hated every minute of it.'

'But what is she *like?* As a person, I mean.'

Roger frowned. 'You'll think I'm crazy, but after all these years I'm not sure I know. I always think of her as the most cosmopolitan woman, though she and André haven't done too much traveling. Doctors don't have time for long trips. That's one of the disadvantages you'll have to live with, honey. Anyway, Dolores has stayed pretty much on the reservation these last twenty-odd years. She goes into Los Angeles now and then, but that's about the extent of it. Still she's worldly in her quiet way. She knows a lot about clothes and entertaining and, as you can see, about decorating. It's the artist in her, I suppose. She studied painting before she and André were married. Went to some school in the East for a while. Then she gave it up to marry my brother. A year later, when they found they couldn't have children, they adopted Drew.' Roger paused. 'It's funny, but I've never really known whether Dolores is happy. She's a very private person. André can be difficult, moody. Sometimes as abrasive as the Señor. But he's a good man and a great doctor.'

'Is she a Californian?'

'Yes. Her maiden name was Del Cruz. Her family and mine have known each other for generations. She and André practically grew up together. Her parents are dead now, but her father was a business associate of my father's. As I recall, they didn't have money, but the family tree – much as Simon would hate to admit it – has older and better branches than the Trippes'. The Señor cares about things like that. He spends most of his time these days working on the family genealogy. I think we're back to Cortez by now. It's a big deal to him. He's as much concerned about blood lines in people as in horses.'

A sudden thought struck me. 'Roger, is that why your father hates me? Because I have no heritage?'

My husband made an effort to avoid a direct answer. 'Darling, he doesn't hate you. Nobody could. It's just his way.'

'No,' I said, 'you're wrong. He does hate me. Why did he make that awful remark about my rushing you into marriage? And why did you say that there were reasons that everyone understood?'

Roger sighed. 'All right, love, I'll tell you. The Señor had a girl picked out for me, just as he picked out Dolores for André. When I fell in love with you I knew I had to marry you fast, before Simon could figure a way to prevent it. That's why he's angry, Ginny. He thought he had things arranged to suit his idea of a "suitable wife" for me. More good, traceable limbs on the family tree.'

I was stunned. 'But that's medieval thinking! It's feudal! My God, Roger, you're thirty years old. Surely your father couldn't make you marry anyone you didn't love! You're a strong man. I can't believe that you wouldn't have stood up to him even if you hadn't met me. He couldn't force you into anything you didn't want!'

He pulled me onto his lap. 'Now calm down, darling. I'm not saying that he could. I just wasn't taking any chances of you getting away from me. Simon can be diabolical when he's crossed. I damned well wasn't going to give him time to make my life hell while he tried to get his way. He's angry now, but he'll get over it. He'll have to. It's our life, not his.'

I felt a cold chill. Simon Trippe was obsessed with family pride. How outraged he must have been when Roger married a 'nobody.' He must have thought about grandchildren with only 'half a background,' Roger's children. It began to be clear to me now. Drew was adopted, André and Dolores could not give Simon the untainted passports to immortality that he wanted. And now Roger had ruined his chances in a different way. No wonder he was so hostile. The man must be half-mad. Both his sons had failed him, in his eyes. The child of a daughter would not carry his name. His sons were his only hope for the next generation and one had married a barren woman, the other a nameless creature who might come from some unspeakable parentage for all that he – or any of us – knew.

The fleeting thought of a daughter brought me back to the mystery of Lila, the sister Roger had not mentioned until today. The room was almost dark now as we sat together in the big deep chair beside the fireplace. I could hear Rosita stirring in the kitchen, preparing dinner. I didn't want to hear more about this strange family of which I was a part. I wanted to savor my first evening as a bride without tales of demented parents and moody brothers and childless sisters-in-law. And yet I had to know more. It was as though I had fallen into a great spider web with Simon at the centre, encircling us all in inescapable strands of family duty and family secrets.

'Tell me about Lila,' I said quietly. I could feel my husband's body stiffen at the question.

'Sweetheart, it's our wedding night,' he said. 'Haven't we talked about enough unpleasant things?'

'Please,' I said. 'I want to know.'

Roger sighed. 'All right. I suppose I should have told you before. Maybe I was afraid to. Maybe I didn't want to risk anything that could have changed your mind about marrying me. Not that Lila's story is disgraceful, God knows. It's just a subject we all seem to avoid.' He took a deep breath. 'My sister is forty-two years old but she looks and acts like a girl of eighteen. She believes she's eighteen, Virginia. That's when time stopped for her. It's never started up again. She has her own little house and a wonderful woman to care for her, a practical nurse named Miss Miles. Milesy, we call her. They keep to themselves, except for the weekly appearance at Sunday dinner at the big house, the one we all have to make. Most of the time Lila's as ingenuous as a young girl, but once in a while she seems to go off her head. Becomes violent, unmanageable. Thank God for Milesy who watches her constantly. I don't believe Lila really knows who any of us is. She thinks Milesy is her mother.'

I was aghast and overcome with pity. 'But that's the saddest thing I ever heard! What happened to her when she was eighteen?'

'She was riding at the girls' school she attended. Some place in Virginia. She was a superb horsewoman, but she took a terrible spill. Landed on her head. They say she was unconscious for weeks. And when she came to, everything was blotted out by the brain injury. I was just a little kid when it happened, but I remember them bringing her home. That is, Dolores brought her home. They were good friends, and since Dolores was at the school at the same time, she looked after Lila and came back with her. Poor Dolores. It was a helluva responsibility to put on a girl who was only twenty herself. I can see it now. I must have been about six at the time. Lila got to the house and I went running to her. She just looked at me and said, "What a nice little boy. Who are you, little boy?" I ran and hid in the barn and cried. André explained it to me later, but I've never forgotten that moment.'

I held him close. 'Sweetheart, how terrible for you. For all of you. And most of all for Lila.'

He kissed me. 'It's a tragic waste of a life, but it could be worse. Most of the time I'm sure she's quite happy in her timeless existence. She's a girl-woman, poor little Lila. You'll see her tomorrow at dinner, unless it's one of her bad days. You'll be amazed, Virginia. She doesn't look much older than that portrait of her in the family drawing room. She was seventeen when it was painted. Dolores painted it, by the way, before they both went off to school.'

'Maybe I could spend some time with her,' I said.

'No. None of us goes to her house. It's better that way. Milesy never leaves her. She can handle her.'

'But darling, I'm a trained nurse. I know how to handle sick people. Perhaps I could help.'

Roger shook his head. 'You're used to handling sick children. Lila is a full-grown, strong woman. I mean it, Virginia. You never know what she might do.' Suddenly he grinned at me. 'What a helluva way to spend our first hours alone together – talking about my family problems! I suppose Rosita would be shocked if we skipped dinner, wouldn't she?'

'I'll tell her to serve it immediately. By the way, does she sleep in? I didn't see a room for her.'

'No. She lives in quarters over by the stables along with Carmelita and some of the other help. Carmelita has worked for André and Dolores since they were married. Do you suppose we'll be able to say the same thing about Rosita when we've been married more than twenty years?'

'If it's anything like the help situation back home, we'll be lucky to have her for twenty days.'

'It's nothing like "back home." Here the staff is part of the family. Josh Jenkins, out at the stables, has worked for us since he was a boy. Long before I was born. Milesy's been here with Lila for twenty-five years and Mrs. Angus has run the big house just about as long.'

I couldn't resist a little barb. 'Maybe they're afraid that Simon will kill them if they leave.'

'Could be,' Roger said affably. 'Could very well be.'

At one o'clock the next day we presented ourselves at the main house. It was a gloriously clear, warm Sunday in June, but the gloomy mansion was as dark and airless as a tomb. I did not look forward to the 'command performance' at the Senior Trippes'. In fact, I was already angry at Simon over a trivial matter even before we arrived.

Roger and I slept late and had to rush to dress for the mid-day meal. Unthinkingly, I had showered and begun to put on a shirt and slacks when my husband stopped me.

'Sweetheart, I'm sorry, but you'll have to wear a dress. And stockings.'

'In California? At home? On Sunday?'

He looked almost shame-faced. 'The home we're going to doesn't approve of women in pants unless they're riding clothes. I know. It's archaic. But it's part of the game we play here called "Simon says."'

I was too angry to be amused. 'He's ridiculous! We're living on the outskirts of twentieth-century Los Angeles, not in the middle of eighteenth-century Madrid!'

Roger shrugged. 'Okay, love, if you want to invite a confrontation, I'll back you.'

I was ashamed of my pettiness. After all, it was Simon's house we were going to . He had a right, I supposed, to dictate the rules in his own home, but the petty tyranny of the man infuriated me. Fuming inwardly, I put on a linen dress and pantyhose. Thank God I could dress as I liked out of Simon's sight. And that, I promised myself, would be as much as possible.

Only André and Dolores were at the house when we arrived, sitting silently with the elder Trippes in the hushed and darkened drawing room. Simon and André barely acknowledged our arrival, but Natalie Tripppe came forward pleasantly.

'I hope you slept well,' she said.

I must have blushed because everyone except Simon looked amused.

'We had a very good night, Mother,' Roger said gravely. He drew me toward the cool, beautiful woman sitting beside André. 'Dolores, dear, you haven't met Virginia.'

'Hello,' she said. 'Welcome. You're even prettier than Roger described you.'

'Welcome,' she'd said. What a lovely word. The first time anyone except Rosita had made me feel that I was wanted here. I smiled gratefully in response.

'Thank you for the beautiful house,' I said. 'It's perfect. It must have been endless trouble for you.'

'Not at all. I'm glad you like it.'

Simon Trippe's voice interrupted the pleasantries.

'Where's Drew? Confound it, André, can't that boy ever be on time?'

'He'll be along in a minute, Father. He's been skeet shooting this morning. He had to change.'

I looked inquiringly at Roger.

'There's a skeet range down the road,' he explained. 'Handling guns, like handling horses, is part of the Trippe education. Have you done any shooting, dear?'

I shook my head. 'I hate guns. I'm terrified of them.'

'So am I,' Dolores said. 'But you get used to them in this family. Everbody's a crack shot around here. No exceptions for sex. Even Mrs. Angus and Miss Miles can hit a tin can at two hundred yards.'

During this small talk I found myself watching the door. I was anxious to meet Drew, but I was even more curious about Lila. I hoped this was one of her 'good days.' Even as I thought it, a young girl, only slightly older looking than the portrait over the fireplace, came into the room. She was followed by a woman in her late forties whom I took to be the faithful Milesy. Lila did, indeed, have the face and figure of a young adult, the graceful yet slightly awkward movements of recently passed adolescence. She *can't* be forty-two, I thought. Time had certainly stood still for her in every way. Roger took my hand and together we approached Lila.

'Hello, Lila dear,' he said. 'It's Roger, remember? I'm so glad to see you again.'

She looked confused. 'Roger? You can't be Roger. He's a little boy.'

'No, I'm all grown up now. I'm a doctor. And this is my wife, Virginia.'

She seemed not to hear the last sentence. Instead, she drew back fearfully. 'I don't like doctors. I'm not sick.' Her voice began to rise hysterically. 'You'll do bad things to me.' Like a child she buried her face in Milesy's shoulder.

'Hush,' the companion said. 'This is your brother, dear. Just like André. He's a doctor, too. You know that. You know it's just the family. No one will hurt you. Milesy won't let them.'

The soothing, possessive voice seemed to calm Lila. Timidly, she raised her head and looked at me.

'How old are you?' she asked.

'I'm twenty-four.'

Lila smiled as though nothing had happened. 'I'm eighteen but I look older, don't you think? Will you come visit me sometime? I have some good records. Glenn Miller and Tommy Dorsey. Do you like them?'

Before I could answer, Drew Trippe burst into the room, his entrance precipitating an outburst of anger from Simon.

'By God, young man, you're an affront to this family! Punctuality is the mark of breeding. If you can't learn to be on time you can have your dinner in the servants' dining room! You act like one so you may as well eat like one!'

A look of pure hatred came over the boy's

handsome face.

'If all the servants in this family ate together, you'd be alone at the dinner table, Grandfather.'

'Drew!' André's voice cut through the room like a whip. 'Apologize to your grandfather at once!'

'I don't want his apology,' Simon Trippe said. 'You'd do better to give me yours, André. You and Dolores. For raising such a disrespectful child. The Trippes are not rude to their elders. Not,' he said pointedly, '*real* Trippes.'

Drew seemed ready to make an angry retort but a little signal from Dolores stopped him. He retreated sullenly to a chair and stayed there silently until Natalie summoned us to dinner.

I found myself seated between Roger and Drew at the enormous, baronial dining table. For a moment I studied the almost aristocratic head that seemed to be tan all over. The eyes were a deep brown, the skin bronzed from the sun, the cropped hair (cut unfashionably short at Simon's demand I guessed) was streaked with natural highlights, the mark of the outdoorsman. He was an extraordinarily good-looking young man. Only his sullen, rebellious expression kept him from being irresistible. Certainly he had spirit. The way he had lashed out at his grandfather was proof of that.

'I'm Virginia. Roger's wife,' I finally said softly. 'We weren't introduced.'

The face that turned to me was suddenly unreadable. 'Good luck,' he said.

I choose to misunderstand. 'Thank you,' I said innocently. 'How was the shooting this morning?'

He acted as though he hadn't heard me. Instead, he insolently studied the faces at the table. 'Nine little Indians,' he said. 'Funny. There should be ten.'

At that moment Roger touched my arm and said something about taking a drive after dinner. Drew seemed relieved that our conversation had ended. During the rest of the meal he did not speak again. For that matter almost nobody did. Roger and André dropped casual remarks, most of them addressed to Simon who offered only terse replies. He was still, obviously, very angry. The women at the table kept silent. Only Lila was unaware of the tension. She chattered girlishly to Milesy whom she called 'Mom.' I could not help noticing that whenever this happened Natalie Trippe tensed almost imperceptibly in her chair at the foot of the table.

It seemed like an endless meal but it was over at last and Roger and I were able to escape into the warm, comforting sunshine. As soon as we were in the car, I turned to Roger.

'Why was your father so hateful to Drew?'

Roger made light of it. 'That little flare-up before dinner, you mean? Think nothing of it. The Señor expects everbody to be on time, that's all.'

I wouldn't be put off. 'Roger, don't treat me like a child. They detest each other. It's because Drew's adopted, isn't it? That's why Simon treats him like a menial. He can't stand anybody whose blood might not possibly be blue, can he? I don't know why you're all so frightened of that old man. He's so obsessed with this family thing I think he's less sane than poor Lila.'

My husband slammed on the brakes so abruptly that I almost went through the windshield. His face was beet-red with rage.

'Don't ever say a thing like that again! No one in this family is insane. Not Lila and certainly not my father! He's eccentric, even tyrannical, but he's strong and brilliant and proud. You're so hung up about being an adopted child yourself that it colors your thinking about everything! I don't want to hear any more about Simon or Drew or Lila. And I don't want you wearing that damned baby ring all the time, either. Even if nobody sees it but me! You're Mrs. Roger Trippe now. You have a name, an identity and an obligation to fit into this family without a lot of sick, nagging questions about hatred and insanity. It's all in your head, Virginia. You've got to learn to curb that vivid imagination or it will destroy you!'

I was speechless. Then slowly, though I tried to stop them, tears began to roll down my face. I had never seen this side of Roger, this angry, violent man who gave orders. I felt cold all over, the way I'd felt when we drove through the big iron gates, the way I had felt more than once since then. And yet my tears were not those of fright. I was crying out of frustration and loneliness and a terrible sense of disappointment in the man I loved.

Roger sat silently, his great, beautiful hands gripping the steering wheel. And then as suddenly as he'd lost his temper he was filled with remorse. He gathered me gently into his arms, kissing away the tears.

'Darling, I'm sorry. Please forgive me. We've both been under a terrible strain these last few days. Maybe we're having newlywed jitters. We seem to be blowing up everything out of proportion. Say you forgive me? I behaved like a beast. It must be hell for you, being thrown into the middle of a big family full of such disparate personalities.' He held me gently. 'I've always heard that a honeymoon is the most difficult time of adjustment in a marriage. Do you think we've broken some kind of a record – married less than two days and already we've had our first fight?'

I tried to smile as I softened under the sincere apology. Of course he was right. This was a new and frightening world, that was all. I wasn't used to the quarrels that were inevitable in a big family. And Roger was probably right, too, about my obsession with adopted children. Still I could not shake off the feeling that something evil permeated the air at Madrugada. I was not imagining an undercurrent of secrecy and hatred that went deeper than perhaps even Roger knew.

'I love you,' I said. 'Let's go home. I gave Rosita the rest of the day off. We'll be lazy and all by ourselves and I'll fix a light snack for supper.'

He grinned at me, happy to be forgiven. 'Don't tell

me you can cook!'

'Never burned a biscuit in my life. Comes from growing up in a servantless household. Anyway, nurses learn to do a lot of things besides bring bedpans!'

He shook his head admiringly. 'I have got to be the world's luckiest man. A beautiful wife who can feed me and take my temperature . . . to say nothing of running it up!'

I felt almost light-hearted as I went to our room to change into comfortable clothes. My only sad moment was when I took the little gold chain and ring from around my neck and dropped it reluctantly into the dresser drawer. I hadn't parted with it since I was seven years old. Before I closed it away I looked at it closely again, hoping once more to discover some secret meaning. But there was nothing but a thin circle of gold set with a line of tiny precious and semi-precious stones: emerald, peridot, pearl, ivory, ruby and turquoise. An old-fashioned ring. One that I would save for our first daughter.

Chapter Three

I SLEPT late the next morning. It was after nine when I opened my eyes to find Roger, fully dressed, standing beside our bed and smiling down at me.

'So this is how it's going to be,' he teased. 'The hard-working doctor off to his clinic while his gorgeous, lazy wife lies in bed.'

I sat up quickly. 'Oh, darling, I'm sorry! Are you ready to leave? What about breakfast?'

'Rosita fed me an hour ago. And don't look so guilty. You can't imagine how masculine it makes me feel to see you there all helpless and dependent while I go off to face the kindergarten killers.'

I was tempted to mention that I'd like to go with him, to feel useful, but it was too late this morning. Tonight, I thought. I'll discuss it with him tonight.

'I'll leave the car for you,' he said. 'You may want to do a little exploring. No problem for me. The clinic is only fifteen minutes away and I'll ride with André. Wil Wiseman will have his car there too, so there'll be plenty of transportation during the day. By the way,

Ginny, would you mind if I invited Wil to dinner tonight? I'm anxious for you two to know each other.'

'That would be fine. I'm dying to meet him.'

'All right, I'll call you after I check with him. Of course he may not be free on such short notice. He's a bachelor, poor devil, and you know what their social calendars are like.' Roger kissed me lingeringly. 'By God, I never thought I'd see the day I wasn't anxious to rush off to my job. Especially my first day in private practice.'

I smiled at him lovingly. 'I'm glad,' I said. 'Good luck, Doctor. Don't let the little monsters eat your stethoscope.'

He seemed to hesitate. 'What do you think you'll do today?'

'I don't know. Explore, I suppose, as you said. I haven't really seen anything of the place. You're not afraid I'll get lost, are you?'

'Mind reader!' He handed me a neatly drawn map, 'Here you go, my girl. I've marked the stable, pool, tennis court and all the houses. Don't get too far off the beaten paths, love. There are apt to be small-game hunters in the woods. Kids, mostly. It's illegal for them to come on the property, but sometimes they do.'

I was half-amused. 'What would they do – mug me, rape me or shoot me?'

'I'm not kidding, Virginia. This is a big place. Stay within the immediate confines, okay?'

'Of course, darling.' I looked at the map. 'I promise

I won't go any farther than the stables.'

He nodded, satisfied. 'Have a good day. Give my best to Josh when you see him.'

I pulled on a shirt and pants and wandered out to the kitchen. Rosita seemed surprised to see me. She had a bed tray set up with delicate china and a pink rosebud from the garden.

'Good morning, Señora. I was waiting to bring you your breakfast.'

'Thank you, Rosita, but the only time I've ever had breakfast in bed was when I was sick. I'll just take toast, juice and coffee. Would you bring it to the patio?'

It was delicious to sit in the sunshine in my own garden, waiting for my morning meal. Creamy pink roses climbed a trellis that screened the patio from the road, bougainvillia and wisteria clung lovingly to the sides of my house. The day was already warm and the sky blue and cloudless. I had a sense of peace and gratitude, thinking of Roger, of the babies who one day would play in this idyllic setting. All the mysteries of yesterday seemed far away as I studied the map that Roger had drawn for me. It seemed that though each area had a sense of privacy, none of the houses were really too far apart. Everything was curiously arranged in a circle, almost, I thought, like the wagon trains which used to act as a fortress against the Indians.

The idea was so ridiculous that it made me smile. Actually, the compound was planned for convenience, and yet the inhabitants had a sense of being on their own land. Beyond the living and working dwellings spread hundreds of acres of unexplored, unused land and trees – insurance that the Trippes would not be troubled by the intrusion of land developers or commercial builders.

Rosita arrived with the tray and the news that the Señor was bringing Dr. Wiseman to dinner.

'Good,' I said. 'Will you plan the menu, please? I'm sure you have a better idea than I of what kind of food Californians prefer. Do you know Dr. Wiseman's preferences?'

'No, Señora, but Carmelita does. She'll help me. Dr. Wiseman used to come to dinner often there.'

'Used to? Doesn't he go there any more?'

Rosita hesitated. 'I think not for a long while, Señora.' Then, as though she was afraid of saying too much, she abruptly took another tack. 'We order the food by telephone, Señora, unless you prefer to drive into the village.'

I let the subject of Wil Wiseman drop. Even I, so simply brought up, knew better than to gossip with servants. 'Order by phone today, please,' I said. 'I'm going to drive around and see the sights.' I held out the map to her. 'The Señor gave me a plan. Did he forget anything?'

She studied it carefully. 'No, Señora, I think it is all here. Except . . .'

'Except what? Is something missing?'

'Only the little house on Señor André's land. It is of

no consequence.'

'What kind of little house?'

'I think you call it a studio. But it has been closed up for many years. Carmelita told me that Señora Dolores used it long ago for her painting. No one goes there now. Carmelita does not even clean it.'

In a few minutes I was in the car, driving slowly in the direction of the stables which I'd decided would be my first stop. I seemed to have a strong pull in that direction. Back home I'd ridden once or twice, very inexpertly, in Rock Creek Park. I was no horsewoman but I was eager to become one and certain that I would be good at the sport.

About half a mile on another road I passed a well-kept, stucco house painted pink. Like ours, it was one-story and sprawling, but from the outside it looked much older and bigger. From the map I knew this was where André and Dolores lived. A few hundred yards behind, almost hidden by trees, I could make out a tiny building which must be the abandoned studio. There was no sign of life anywhere as I drove slowly by, admiring the simple architectural lines of the graceful house and the pleasing, artistic planting which surrounded it.

Turning, according to directions, onto still another road I drove for perhaps ten or fifteen minutes before I saw the stables and living quarters for the employees. It was an impressive sight. There were several big red-and-white barns and a small cluster of cottages. In the huge paddock at least a dozen horses grazed contentedly. To my eyes they were all beauties, sleek chestnut creatures who occasionally stopped nibbling the grass to gallop the length of the big enclosure in high spirits or nuzzle each other delightedly like great, playful children.

I don't know how long I sat there, entranced. I felt strangely at home, almost as though I'd been transported back to another time. I was so absorbed that I did not even notice the man who came up to the convertible from behind it. I literally jumped when he put his face near mine and said, 'Morning, ma'am. You must be Dr. Roger's wife.'

I looked into the kindest eyes I'd ever seen, eyes that were almost the same blue-violet color as my own. The sun glinted in those eyes and illuminated a tanned, strong, attractively lined face. I judged him to be anywhere between forty-five and sixty. I couldn't tell, for the hair was snow-white, yet the face was young, furrowed not from age but from constant exposure to the outdoors. He had on well-worn riding breeches and boots and a sport shirt open at the throat. And his smile offered the warmest, most irresistible kind of welcome.

We shook hands. 'You're Mr. Jenkins,' I said.

'Josh,' he corrected. 'Very pleased to know you, Mrs. Trippe. Dr. Roger's a lucky man.'

'Virginia,' I said in turn, holding onto the big, rough, yet surprisingly gentle grasp. He seemed pleased. 'Thank you,' he said, releasing my hand. 'You like horses.'

It was a statement, not a question.

'I don't really know anything about them, but yes, I like them. I hope you'll teach me to ride if you can spare the time. Roger says you're the best instructor in the world.'

'Well, I don't know about that, but I got him to the point where he didn't fall off very often. Anyway, it'd be a pleasure to teach you. Like to have a look around? Come on, I'll introduce you to my babies.'

Like two kids we hung over the paddock fence as the beautiful animals came up to have their muzzles rubbed and to accept the cubes of sugar that Josh showed me how to offer them, flat, on the palm of my hand. We toured the stables and ended up in the tack room which was lined with glass cases filled with ribbons and silver trophies, the latter all meticulously shined and many bearing inscriptions that went back more than thirty years. I examined them with interest. Quite a few were inscribed to Lila Trippe. It was a marvelous display and I complimented Josh on their beautiful condition.

'They're the proudest things in my care,' he said, 'those trophies and the horses out there. I'm a sentimental, crusty old bachelor, Virginia, but when I look at those animals and remember the ones who came before them, I feel like I've raised a family. Sometimes,' he said with a laugh, 'I almost forget that everything at Madrugada really belongs to Mr. Simon.'

'Including the family,' I said, almost thinking

aloud.

Josh gave me a half-pitying look. 'I see you've met the Señor. Of course. Yesterday was Sunday, wasn't it?'

We exchanged knowing looks and I thought I saw sympathy on his face. He knows what a devil Simon is. He understands how I feel even better than Roger does. But then he would. Josh, after all, was not a member of the family. He'd been part of it longer than my own husband, but he didn't have the blind devotion that was inbred in Simon Trippe's son.

'I see Lila's name on so many of the old trophies,' I said.

Josh's face saddened. 'She was the best. Even as a kid she could outride and outjump any of us. I remember the last horse she had. Beautiful little mare, full of spirit.' His voice became almost wistful. 'But not as much spirit as Lila had. They were a pair you'd never forget. Lila was so beautiful on that proud little filly. Virginia Dare, Lila named her. God, how she loved her! I think Lila hated to leave Virginia Dare even more than she hated to leave the rest of us when she went away to school.'

'How tragic that the sport she loved most was the thing that destroyed her,' I said.

Josh shook his head. 'I'll never understand it. I'd have bet there wasn't a horse alive that Lila couldn't handle. She took a spill now and then, like everybody does. But one of the things she knew best was how to get clear.' He fell silent. Then he said, 'It's crazy, you know, but sometimes I almost believe she didn't fall. That maybe it was some other kind of accident. Of course, we'll never really know.'

'But Dolores was there,' I said. 'She knew what happened.'

'Yes, of course,' Josh said. 'Miss Dolores was there. I guess I've just never been able to accept it. Maybe in some mixed up way I think it was my fault, something I forgot to teach Lila, something I overlooked.'

I put my hand on his arm. 'Josh, you know better than that. The most experienced riders get badly hurt, even killed.'

'Yes, I know. With my mind I know. With my heart I'll always wonder.' Abruptly he seemed to shake off his memories. 'Well, now, I don't know what makes me so gabby this morning! Must be you. It's been so long since I've seen a pretty young lady around here. You remind me a lot of Lila when she was a few years younger than you. Takes me back. Say, how about a cup of coffee? Got some on the stove in my quarters upstairs. That is, if you don't think we'd be gossiped about, being alone in my apartment.' The last was said with such a twinkle that I laughed.

'I'll risk it,' I said solemnly, 'if you will.'

Josh led the way upstairs and excused himself to get the coffee from the tiny kitchenette. I wandered curiously around the small living room. It was filled with books of horsemanship and photographs of steeplechase riders taking soaring, breathtaking hurdles. There were a few of Josh himself, holding silver cups. But there was only one picture of a girl sitting quietly astride a horse. The photograph was old but the girl was obviously Lila. An unshakeable conviction spread over me. Josh had been in love with Lila and perhaps she with him. Had Simon known that his precious daughter was in love with the riding master? Was that why she was shipped off to school in the East? And was she so miserable there that she did not avoid – or maybe even provoked – an accident to get back to Josh? There was something mysterious about the fact that the family had not gone to her. That they had left it all to Dolores was out of character even for parents as respectively cold and frightened as Simon and Natalie Trippe. What did Josh suspect? Something. He had made that clear in his brief but unexpectedly candid conversation about the accident.

Stop it! I scolded myself. Just because you feel sorry for Lila, like Josh, and hate Simon you're building a fantasy out of a sad but quite possible occurrence. It was absurd to think that Simon was breaking up a love affair between Lila and Josh. In the normal course of events a girl like Lila Trippe would have been sent East to a finishing school. Besides, if Simon had any idea of attachment, he'd have fired Josh on the spot. I was romanticizing because I felt affection for two unfortunate people.

But one thing I was sure of. Josh Jenkins *had* once cared deeply for Lila Trippe. And from the way he sounded, he still did.

When he returned with the coffee, we talked of

other things. Born in this beautiful, expansive country, he had the native's unflagging enthusiasm for all that his state offered – its relaxed way of life, its lack of pressure and tension, its semi-tropical climate.

'You sound like the Chamber of Commerce,' I teased. 'Come on, Josh, there must be some *bad* things about Southern California.'

He smiled, the craggy face wrinkling into an expression of indulgent amusement.

'Well, we have a couple of minor problems,' he said. 'The smog gets pretty bad in town, and it has been known to hit us even out here. And there's the rainy season. It doesn't come often, but I'll admit that when it hits – like in January – I'd trade the stables for Noah's Ark.' He sobered. 'Of course, the worst thing we have to fear is fire. When the Santa Ana blows, Southern California can lose hundreds of houses and thousands of acres of forests. One little spark in the woods can erupt into a raging inferno in minutes when that devil decides to help it along.'

'What's the Santa Ana? I've never heard of it.'

'It's a meteorological nightmare peculiar to this part of the world. A strong, hot, dusty wind from the inland desert region. It comes barreling to the Pacific Coast around Los Angeles. When we've had a dry spell and a little fire starts, the force of the Santa Ana is more than man can reckon with.'

We chatted idly for a few more moments and then Josh saw me to my car, the smart little convertible with the top down, evidence of my new, affluent way of life. We made a date to start my riding lessons the next morning. I was pleased by the prospect.

Still reviewing my visit with Josh, I decided to take a little drive into the wooded area beyond the stables. The trees looked so cool and inviting. I could not visualize them angrily ablaze. I would drive as far as I could, then walk a little way into the deep greenery, maybe sit under a tree and try to put my thoughts into focus. In spite of my pleasant visit with Josh, I felt troubled for no reason that I could clearly analyze.

I started the car and began to drive slowly toward the woods, my thoughts full of Lila and Josh, comparing the innocent sweetness of the woman and the gentle kindness of the man to the anger of Simon, the aloofness of André, the hostility of Drew. I thought of the cool composure of Dolores and the obviously nervous, agitated attitude of my mother-in-law. What a strange family it was! Each of them almost guarded in his reaction to me. Even my darling Roger had shown an angry, defensive side of his nature yesterday.

Again I told myself that it was only the strangeness of it all. I would adjust to them and they to me. Roger and I would have a long, full, happy life together.

But even as I formed the words in my mind, the life I pictured nearly came to an end. As I rounded a heavily wooded curve in the road a sharp noise rang out and a hole cut cleanly through the windshield, missing me by inches. Instinctively I slammed on the brakes and threw myself flat on the seat of the car.

There was nothing now but silence and the bullet hole with its spreading web of cracks. Cautiously, I raised my head. There were no more shots. Those damned kids! Roger had warned me about stray hunters, but I'd forgotten. More angry than alarmed, I jumped out of the car and looked around. There was no one in sight. There wouldn't be, of course. Probably they were more frightened than I. I walked a few feet in the woods. Nothing.

'Hey!' I yelled. 'Do you know you almost killed sombody? Get off this property!'

Nothing stirred. Not so much as a leaf. Then a glint of red caught my eye. It was a cheap red cotton bandana, the Western cowboy variety. Everyone from boys to old men wore them with sports clothes. I had noticed a great many on men in the village last Saturday as we drove through on our way to Madrugada. Feeling foolish, as though I were playing amateur detective, I picked it up. It was like a thousand others except for one thing. In the corner was a single letter embroidered in black. And the letter was 'T.'

Delayed reaction set in. My knees shook so badly at the realization of my near-death that I could barely keep my foot on the gas pedal on the drive home. Suddenly I was not sure that the bullet hole was from the gun of a stray poacher.

I was almost fainting as I finally entered my own house. Rosita, who came forward to greet me, looked frightened. I was trembling violently and my face must have been stark white.

'Señora! What is the matter? Are you sick?'

I shook my head numbly. 'I was driving. Near woods. A bullet hit the car. Almost killed me.' The tears came at last, I began to cry hysterically.

Rosita led me to the living room couch, making little calming noises. 'It is bad, Señora,' she said. 'The hunters. They are all over the property. You must not go so far from the buildings. The Señor will be upset.' She eased me onto the sofa and spread a light robe over me. 'I make you a drink, yes? Tea? A brandy? Do you wish me to call the Señor?'

'No, no. I'm all right. It was stupid of me.' I lay back, closing my eyes, trying to calm myself. The hysteria had passed and I could see how foolish I'd been. Roger had specifically warned me about this. He'd be alarmed and angry. Then I realized I was still clutching the bandana.

'Rosita,' I said, 'have you ever seen a scarf like this before?'

'Of course, Señora. Many of them. All the men wear them. Even some of the women.'

'But look,' I said, 'this one has an initial.'

She inspected it closely and then smiled. 'But there are many of those, too, Señora. My aunt, Carmelita, embroiders them for the family. Every year at Christmas she gives six to each of us. Even the people who work here. We are all very proud to have our bandanas which say we are part of the rich Trippe family.'

I was amazed. '*Everyone* has bandanas like these?'

'Oh, yes, Señora. From Señor Simon to the little boy who cleans the stables. Carmelita is very generous.' Rosita giggled. 'She says she must make many because we are always losing them or throwing them away or using them for cleaning rags. You see, Señora, the scarf cost nothing. It is only Carmelita's work that makes them special.'

'I see,' I said. 'Thank you, Rosita. I'll rest a while before I change. What time did the Señor say that he and Dr. Wiseman would get here?'

'About seven o'clock. But it is only two o'clock now, Señora. Shall I fix lunch for you?'

'No,' I said. 'I'm not hungry. I think I'll go into my room and rest awhile.'

Still holding the bandana, I went into our bedroom, undressed and lay down. It was only coincidence that I'd found the scarf so near to where the shot had come from. It could have been there for days, dropped by any one of fifty people in the compound who owned identical ones. It had to be an accidental bullet from a stranger's gun that had crashed through the windshield. It was unthinkable that someone had deliberately aimed at me and that the would-be assassin had dropped the bandana in his – or her – flight. Melodrama seemed to be becoming my specialty. Impatient with my own imaginings, I wadded up the kerchief and threw it across the room. And yet a small suspicion lingered. Was Rosita telling the truth? Did everybody in the compound own initialed red bandanas? Feeling like a fool, I got up and went to the dresser drawer where Roger kept his scarves and ascots. Sure enough, there was a neatly folded pile of red bandanas, all identical to the one I'd found in the woods. I was sure that the same collection would be found in every bureau drawer in every house and cottage and room in Madrugada. It proved nothing. The only lesson to be learned was the one Roger had tried to teach me that morning: Stay close to the heart of the compound.

But what if someone did want me out of the way for some reason I could not imagine? I would not be safe anywhere. Not if there really was someone who hated or feared me enough to want me dead.

It was an accident, I told myself over and over. An accident. I drifted into an exhausted sleep. In my dream I was being strangled by a red bandana. I could not see who stood behind me drawing the fabric tighter and tighter around my throat. I could not see whether the hands were those of a man or a woman. Only that they relentlessly, silently were choking the life out of me. My own screams awakened me. Rosita cam running into the room.

'Señora! What is it?'

Half-awake, I said, 'Someone was trying to murder me.'

The girls expression of terror brought me back to my senses. 'In my *dream*,' I explained. 'I was having a *nightmare*,' I managed to laugh. 'I didn't know that life was so dangerous in the Wild West, Rosita. I thought people only got shot at in cowboy movies.'

Chapter Four

BY THE time Roger came home, bringing Wilson Wiseman, I had convinced myself that the shooting was only a frightening but unintentional error, and the bandana simply an unrelated prop that happened to have been carelessly dropped, at some earlier time, near the scene. I hoped that on his way in Roger would not even look at the car with its telltale bullet hole. I felt like a foolish, hysterical woman. I would tell him about it when we were alone. It was not the note on which I wished to meet my husband's associate.

My hopes were realized. The two men obviously had not looked at the car which I'd left in front of our house. Roger was bubbling with high spirits as he preceded Wil into the living room where I was waiting, the cocktails and canapes already set out for them.

'Here she is, Wil,' he said. '*Now* will you agree that I didn't overstate the case?'

I was not prepared for Dr. Wilson Wiseman. I had pictured him as the senior member of the team, a much older man than either of the brothers, probably nearer Simon's age than their own. Instead I came face to face with a handsome, dark-haired, vital man who couldn't have been more than a year or two older than André. If Hollywood were to cast the urbane, polished medical man, it could have done no better than Wil. What a handsome trio they must make in their clinic, I thought. The good-looking blond Trippe brothers and this sexy-looking brunette bachelor. I could imagine the local mothers looking forward to their visits to the pediatricians.

Through cocktails and dinner, Wil seemed to be watching me carefully. But it was a friendly observation, as though he cared about my happiness and well-being and was truly glad that Roger and I were married. Perhaps he was also weighing my ability to adjust to my new situation. He must know the Trippes very well. It was Wilson who had first set up practice in the area and, two years later, had taken in André when he finished his medical training. Now he was doing the same for Roger and I was glad that my exuberant young husband would be working side by side with this easy, attractive man.

Roger was full of his first day at the clinic. 'I was as nervous as a pre-med student,' he said, 'but I guess I muddled through.'

'You're going to be good,' Wilson assured him. 'You've had fine training and your bedside – or should I say cribside? – manner is better than André's or mine.' He turned to me. 'You can be very proud of him, Virginia. He knows what he's doing and the kids adore him. You should see them relax when he gets hold of them.'

I felt very happy, and Roger seemed pleased, though he laughed deprecatingly at Wil's praise.

'I don't know whether I'm good or just the new patsy,' he said. 'Those guys ran my ass off today. I was elected to make house calls this afternoon and they've had the nerve to put me on call tonight. How do you like that, honey? First day and I've got the night duty! Let's hope there isn't a midnight epidemic of tonsilitis!'

We were back in the living room. Roger poured brandy for Wil and me, took orange juice for himself. 'Just in case,' he explained. 'That damned phone might ring any minute. By the way, love, what did you do today?'

I felt so thoroughly at ease that I was almost tempted to tell them about the stray shot, making a joke of it. But instead I said, 'I spent a lot of time at the stables. Josh is terrific. He gave me the full tour and promised to start my lessons tomorrow.'

'Hey, that's great!' Roger looked delighted. 'You didn't wander too far away from the main area, did you? The stables are as far as I want you to go.'

Before I could answer I was saved by the ringing of the phone. His voice was very calm as he talked to a distraught mother. 'All right, Mrs. Collins. I'm sure there's nothing to worry about, but if his temperature is that high I'd better hop over and take a look.' He hung up and turned apologetically to me. 'A taste of things to come. But I shouldn't be too long. Keep her company, Wil. That is, if I can trust you alone with my bride.'

Wiseman smiled. 'Don't count on it. You know my reputation. Why do you think I made sure you were on call tonight?'

'I'm flattered,' I said, laughing. But Roger did not seem amused by the flirtatious little joke. He couldn't possibly be jealous!

'You were smart to marry a nurse, darling,' I said. 'At least I understand that when you're making a house call you're *really* calling on a house where somebody is sick.'

My attempt at lightness fell flat. A peculiar expression crossed Wil's face. It was then that I realized that Roger was going to take our car. He'd see the windshield and wonder what had happened. He'd be angry for sure. And he had a right to be. I followed him to the door.

'Dear, there's something I should tell you,' I said. 'About today.'

He kissed me hurriedly. 'Not now, honey. Be back shortly.'

'But Roger . . .' No use. He was halfway down the path. In the dark it might be some time before he saw the damaged windshield. Reluctantly, I returned to the living room.

'Something wrong?' Wil asked.

I blurted out the story of the accident. 'Roger will

kill me when he sees that bullet hole,' I said. 'I should have told him immediately.'

Wil looked troubled. 'You were foolish to take chances driving into those lonely woods. And *more* foolish to get out of the car afterwards. My God, child, what did you think you were going to find?'

'I don't know,' I said miserably. 'I wasn't thinking at all, I suppose. After the first fright I was so angry at those poachers that I wanted to tell them what their damned stray bullet had nearly done. But of course they'd run off. Or maybe the shot came from so far away that they didn't even know they'd almost hit me.'

'In any case, there was no trace of them?'

'No. Nothing. That is, nothing but an old red bandana caught on a bush.'

'A red bandana with an initial embroidered on it?'

I looked at him startled. 'Yes. How did you know?'

'It's a Trippe trademark. Everybody here has them. There must be hundreds around, made by Carmelita over the years. Even *I* used to wear one. Years ago. When I spent more time here than I do now. You're likely to find them everywhere – from around Simon's neck to the rag bag in your own cleaning room.'

'I know. That's what Rosita told me.' We were silent for a moment. 'Anyway,' I said, 'I was dumb to put myself in the line of fire today. I'll never do it again. I had to learn the hard way.'

'Most of us do,' Wil said.

I longed to ask him why he didn't come to the Trippe compound any more. I had a hunch that it was because of Simon. Probably he couldn't stand the old man any more than I could. But why did he no longer visit André and Dolores?

As though I said her name aloud, Wil suddenly changed the subject. 'The house is charming,' he said. 'How did Roger manage to get this dreary place transformed into something that suits you so well?'

'Dolores did it before we arrived.'

Wil smiled. 'I should have guessed. Who else around here would have the taste or the interest?' He took a sip of his drink. 'Well, now, why don't we level with each other, Virginia? You tell me your impressions of the Trippe clan, and I'll tell you mine.'

I hesitated, eager to talk yet reluctant to sound disloyal in front of someone I hardly knew. Even though I'd warmed immediately to Wil and felt instinctively that I could trust him, he was an 'outsider.' It seemed out of order to criticize my in-laws even to one who had once apparently been almost like a member of the family. Instead of coming straight out with the things that had troubled me since my arrival, I said inanely, 'Everyone's been very kind.'

Wil gave me a satisfied look. 'You're not only very pretty, you're also very well-mannered. Your parents must have taught you the nicety of the little white lie. But if you tell me that Simon Trippe has been kind to you I shall think you are either a liar or an insensitive clod. And I know that you are neither.'

I didn't answer.

'I suppose you think I'm prying,' Wil said. 'A nosy old bachelor, wondering what's going on. I don't have to wonder, Virginia. I know without anyone having to tell me. Simon has given you a hard time. It would have to be that way. He hasn't an ounce of kindness or compassion in his whole arrogant body. For that matter, neither has André. They're two of a kind. Cold, dispassionate, mechanical men.'

His last words shocked me. The criticism of Simon was so obvious that I was not surprised Wil saw through my polite little evasion. But to attack André, who I thought was his close friend and partner? It seemed a reckless thing to do. What if I repeated his words to Roger or to André?

'Don't look so horrified,' Wil said. 'Everyone knows what I think of the Trippe men – all of them except your husband. Simon hasn't laid eyes on me in years, and André knows exactly how I feel about him. It doesn't matter to him. André's clinical approach to life has nothing to do with his medical ability. I suppose it enhances it, never feeling emotion about anything. He's a first-rate doctor, which is why I work with him. But I don't have to take him into my personal life. I tried once. I tried to used my head instead of my heart. I wanted even the crumbs at this family table, literally. Used to come to those ghastly Sunday dinners. But no more. Not for years.'

I remembered Drew's odd remark about 'the tenth

Indian.' Did he mean Wil?

'Do you include Drew in your category of Trippe men?'

'Yes,' Wil said slowly, 'I guess I do. He's a strange boy. A strange boy,' he repeated, 'who is determined to be a Trippe though he has none of their blood. I think he has patterned himself after Simon and André. even though I'm not sure he doesn't hate them.' Wil seemed lost in thought. 'Do you know,' he said suddenly, 'that tonight is the first time I've driven through these gates in almost fifteen years?'

'Fifteen year!' I was aghast.

He nodded. 'It took me a long time to cut my personal ties with the Trippes. I had always looked up to them, almost stood in awe of Simon's power. It was years before I realized that I was being masochistic, that I really was miserable every time I set foot in this brooding, gloomy place. I wouldn't have come tonight except that I wanted to see you. To study you, if you will. And now I'm more concerned than ever. Can you live in this atmosphere, Virginia? Can you survive in an aura of isolation and suspicion?'

For a moment I wondered whether he was mad. I had already felt something of the unhappy picture he painted of Madrugada and the people who inhabited it, and yet I thought Wil was being melodramatic.

'It's not Bluebeard's Castle, Wil,' I said. 'I admit it's not exactly what I'd imagined, but there are good things here, too. Josh is wonderfully kind. And somehow I'm drawn to Lila. I'd like to help her if I could. And Dolores, though I hardly know her, seems a beautiful human being to me. I hope we'll be friends.'

'And is that what you call a life?' Wil's voice was harsh. 'Is it enough to surround yourself with a horse trainer, a mentally retarded creature and a woman who may never let you get close to her?'

'You're forgetting Roger, aren't you?' I asked icily. 'He's the main part of my life, the reason for my being here. We love each other. We'll have babies, a whole life of our own. Maybe,' I said, voicing a thought that I didn't even know was in the back of my mind, 'we'll leave here one day and Roger will set up a practice somewhere else.' My own words surprised and annoyed me, for they confirmed what I had not planned to admit to anyone – that I already hated this place and wished we had never come to it.

Wil poured himself another brandy. He was getting a little drunk, I realized, but he knew exactly what he was saying. Perhaps the liquor had given him the courage to say it.

'That's what I wanted to hear,' he said. 'You work on Roger, Virginia. Make him leave this place, the sooner the better. There are things here that even Roger doesn't know. Remember, he was a late child. He's many years younger than André and Lila. I'm not sure he's aware of half the things that go on, or have gone on, in this family.' He took a sip of his drink. 'I must be getting a little high, judging from my loose tongue. But I care about you. You're very important. I don't want to see you wither and die in this compound. Like some of the others. You're a pretty bird who needs to be free. And they won't permit that.'

He had given me the opening I needed. 'Wil, I'd like to work at the clinic until I get pregnant. Would you be in favor of that?'

'Of course. Why not? We could use you and it would be good for you. But have you discussed it with Roger?'

'No. Not yet.'

'He'll turn you down. Trippe mentality. Even Roger has some of it. Their women are secluded Señoras, exclusively their own property. They don't get out to be contaminated by the outside world. You've seen Natalie and Dolores. Do you get any feeling of independent, emancipated women? Now Lila was different. She defied her father. And look at her.'

'Wil, what really happened to Lila? You must have been close to the family at the time.'

'I'm sure you've heard the story.' It was a flat answer that meant, 'keep your nose out of that one.' I went back to the subject of my working at the clinic.

'I can't really believe that Roger will object to my helping out. I'm a trained nurse. We met when we were doing the same kind of work! Even you said that he's different from his father and André. He couldn't possibly be made to share their outmoded views about women.'

'He can be made to do anything Simon wants,' Wil said. 'He's no different in that respect than any of the others.'

I heard the front door slam. A furious Roger stormed into the room.'Virginia! What the hell is a bullet hole doing in the car?' He shook me violently by the shoulders, ignoring Wil. 'Where did you go today? What in God's name happened?'

Haltingly, I gave him the explanation, apologizing for ignoring his warning to me, promising never to do it again. He scolded me and then held me close, forgiving me and making me promise to stay always within view of the houses of the stables. I agreed eagerly, anxious to have the whole episode forgotten.

When I raised my head from my husband's chest, Wil had disappeared. Somewhere early on in my confession he had quietly, discreetly left the house.

The next few days were lonely for me, for I'd been used to a busy, active life. I said nothing to Roger about working at the clinic, though I went one day to see it and felt a longing to be part of the busy, productive atmosphere. I sensed that Wil was right. Roger would not want his wife working anywhere, it was not 'fitting' for a Trippe lady. The almost-respectful attitude of the two nurses confirmed my feeling. They could never accept me as a co-worker. Reluctantly I gave up the idea of being anything more than the wife of Dr. Roger and the mother of his children.

I threw myself passionately into my riding lessons, arriving at the stable early, having lunch there with Josh and becoming familiar with the horses and the fine points of horsemanship. I spent most of the day on horseback, either riding through he woods with Josh as protector-companion, or exercising in the riding ring. I became more and more fond of Josh, though we did not soon return to the subject of Lila. When I tried, once or twice, to bring her name into the conversation he was unresponsive, as though he was sorry that he'd said as much as he had at our first meeting. Instead, he told me long stories of horse shows and competitions. Only once did he mention Lila.

'It was our dream that she show in Madison Square Garden,' he said. 'She and Virginia Dare. It would have been a wonderful moment.'

'Couldn't she ride even now, Josh?' I asked. 'She seems physically fit, and if you were with her nothing could happen, could it?'

'Out of the question. She's not even allowed to visit the stables. Her father's orders. He's probably right, at that. God knows what would happen. Might bring back terrible memories of that accident.'

'But maybe that would be good,' I persisted. 'Maybe she needs to remember.'

He shook his head. 'They say she'll never remember anything. Not in the right way. Seeing horses just might confuse her more, even make her worse. When the brain's been damaged, Virginia, there's no telling what'll trigger an attack.'

'Have you ever seen one of these "attacks"?'

'No, but I've heard about them. Miss Miles has all she can do to handle her when they happen.' He seemed to want to terminate the conversation. 'You've been fooling around with these brutes all week,' he said. 'Got yourself a favorite yet?'

'This one, of course,' I said, patting the chestnut mare I was riding. 'This one is my darling, my little Princess T. We understand each other.'

Josh laughed. 'Guess you can consider her yours, then. Roger said you were to have the one you wanted.'

I was childishly delighted. 'You mean she's really mine? I can own her?'

'Seems like it. Roger said he'd buy the one you picked out from his father, so as you'd feel like she out-and-out belonged to you.'

I hugged Princess T. Maybe you're a bribe, I told her silently. Something to keep me occupied so I won't get bored and restless. But I don't care. You're beautiful and I love you.

'Can I rename her now that she's mine?'

'Well, no, not officially,' Josh said. 'She's registered like all the other of the Trippe stable – Lady T, Señora T, Cabellero T, every one of them. But you can call her anything you want.'

'How about "Virginia Dare"?'

I'd thought I was making a sentimental suggestion. I was not prepared for the pain in Josh's eyes before he turned his back on me.

'Call her anything you like,' he said roughly. 'She'll still be Princess T.'

Chapter Five

THE NEXT two weeks were almost a repetition of the first. Roger and I were happy in our house and Rosita was a joy, but we endured the same dreary Sunday dinners and I continued to live a solitary existence while my husband was at work. It was not really solitary because of Josh and Virginia Dare. But I yearned for company and conversation beyond the stables. Dolores, polite to me at the main house, had made no overtures of friendship. There seemed to be no social exchange between the brothers. And, of course, contact with Lila was forbidden, just as any possible closeness to Natalie was out of the question. I had no desire to risk a confrontation with Simon.

I made a point of passing the pool and the tennis courts daily in the hope of catching a glimpse of Drew. My nephew by marriage was hardly lovable, but he was the only other member of the family anywhere near my own age and I hoped that we might find some common interests, even become friendly. But I never saw him except at Sunday dinner when he was as uncommunicative and sullen as ever.

I wrote long letters, falsely cheerful, to my family back East, dwelling on the beauty of the estate and the excitement of owning and riding my own horse. If they noticed the lack of mention of any of my 'new family' except Roger, they did not comment on it. They replied with long, loving accounts of their days and told me how much them missed me, always emphasizing their happiness at the news of my own.

Wil Wiseman did not come to the house again though I'd asked Roger once or twice to invite him.

'Wil has a busy schedule, darling,' Roger said. 'He's in constant demand socially, and why not? A good-looking, unmarried, successful doctor is chased by every woman in the county, married and unmarried.'

'It's strange he's never married,' I said. 'Did he ever come close?'

'Not to my actual knowledge. I've heard rumors that he was in love once, but it didn't work out. Gossip says he never got over it. Seems pretty Victorian to me, but that's the accepted explanation.' Roger laughed. 'One thing's for sure, I know he likes women. There's no problem that way.'

'But you don't know who the girl was?'

'No. She was a local. That's all I know.'

'What a waste,' I said.

'What a typical feminine reaction,' Roger teased. 'There's a little matchmaker in every woman, isn't there? You're right, of course. He's missing the best part of life. But that's his choice, honey, and none of our business why he chose to make it.'

I debated whether to come out with the thought that had recently crossed my mind. Roger was volatile where his family was concerned, but my idea seemed innocent enough.

'You know,' I said pensively, 'I wonder whether he was in love with Lila. After all, they were all very close when they were young, weren't they? André and Dolores and Wil and Lila? He told me he used to come here often, years ago. Maybe he hoped for Lila's recovery. Maybe it took him years to admit that it was hopeless so he finally stopped coming.'

Roger seemed amused. 'Sweetheart, have you ever thought of writing romantic novels? No, dear, I think you're on the wrong track. If that had been the case, I'd have heard about it somewhere along the way. I'm sure the girl Wil loved was someone none of us knew. Anyway,' he said, dismissing the subject, 'it's ancient history. Wil's nearly fifty. I doubt that he'll ever marry now.'

'He's still a very attractive man.'

A change came over my husband. 'Just don't find him too attractive. Personallly I like him, and I respect him. But don't expect to see too much of him, Virginia. The family doesn't encourage his visits. The Señor and André don't like him any more than he likes them.'

'Oh, you know that!' My impulsive reaction was a dead giveaway.

'Yes. Apparently you do, too. I suppose he told you

so the night he was here.'

I didn't answer.

'Let's forget Wil Wiseman, okay? We have a good professional association, but that's where it ends.'

'I don't understand,' I said. 'Why did you invite him here the first time?'

'I wanted to show you off. Now I have. No need for a repeat performance.'

I didn't believe him. It was more likely that Simon or André or both of them had heard about the dinner and 'suggested' to Roger that he not pursue the social contact with Wil. It seemed to give credence to my hunch that Wil, like Josh, had loved Lila and that his presence somehow threatend the isolation in which that poor woman was kept.

Admittedly, I was curious. But then I had so little to think about these days that even conjecture was a welcome diversion. 'An idle mind is a sick mind,' my mother used to say. And certainly my mind was very little occupied. Maybe Roger was right. Perhaps I should put my fantasies on paper. I seemed to be living in a made-up world, better suited to the pages of a novel than to any sensible reality.

Still, the thought of Lila and Wil stayed with me. My spur-of-the-moment theory about them seemed more and more possible as I considered it. So possible, in fact, that next morning I disobeyed my husband once again. Unannounced, except to tell Rosita where I was going, I went to see Lila.

I had begun to walk everywhere these days. The

exercise was good for me and the distances to the pool, the tennis court and the stables were not too great. Subconsciously, I suppose, I also avoided driving the car except when I had to, unable to forget the time it had almost been the site of my death. For the same reason, I never went near the skeet range where the guns were kept. I might have found Drew there, but I wanted no part of any more shooting, not even when it was for sport.

A brisk half-mile walk brought me to the doll's house where Lila and Milesy lived. All I could think of as I approached it was that it was a fairy-story cottage, snow-white with pale pink shutters, a Hansel and Gretel setting, all dreamlike and innocent, as untouched as its owner. I faltered a little as I approached the door. Perhaps I would be turned away by Milesy, the protective mother tiger. It would be embarrassing and Roger would be angry with me. But something drew me to Lila. Something more than mere curiosity about her and Wil Wiseman. I had a strong sense of identity with this charming, unworldly creature, and a conviction, that wouldn't go away, that she needed me, that I somehow was the only one who wanted to help her.

Summoning all my courage, I knocked on the door. A surprised Milesy opened it and stood there looking at me in undisguised astonishment.

'Good morning,' I said. 'I hope I'm not disturbing you and Lila, but I was out for a walk and I suddenly thought how nice it would be to visit with both of you.'

For a moment I thought she was going to shut the door in my face. But instead she recovered her poise and even managed a half smile.

'Come in,' she said. 'Lila's having a little rest before lunch, but I'm sure she'll be up in a few minutes.' She looked pointedly at her watch. 'It's eleven-thirty,' she said. 'We always lunch promptly at twelve-fifteen.'

So much for the preannounced length of my visit. I knew that an invitation to stay for lunch would not be forthcoming.

Milsey led me into a small living room, one that might have been the sitting room of a young girl's suite. The decor was of the late forties, very 'modernistic' and strangely at odds with the old-world, romantic charm of the exterior. Time had stopped here twenty-five years before, as it had for Lila. I noticed a record player in one corner of the room and, on the walls, photographs of the family and, I presumed, girlhood friends. There were no pictures of horses or riders. And there were none of Josh Jenkins or Wil Wiseman. There were old movie magazines in the bookcase, books by F. Scott Fitzgerald and *Vogues* of 1947.

'You're surprised,' Milesy said flatly.

'No,' I lied, 'not at all. It's charming.'

'It is not charming, Mrs. Trippe. It is the way it was when Lila left it twenty-five years ago. Everything exactly the same. Just as she is exactly the same.'

The cold, unfriendly voice chilled me. I felt like the intruder I was, and I was sorry that I had come. It would be awkward to leave now, but I would make my escape as soon as I decently could. I searched for some topic of conversation while we waited for Lila. My mind was a blank. I felt like a schoolgirl under the scrutiny of the headmistress.

'I hear you've been spending most of your time at the stables,' Milesy said.

'Yes,' I said gratefully, happy to be on safe ground. 'Josh Jenkins has been teaching me to ride.'

'Did he also teach you to name your horse Virginia Dare?'

The remark was like a sharp, swift blow and I reacted to it as I would have to a physical attack. I caught my breath. 'No, of course not,' I said.

'Come, come, Mrs. Trippe. News travels fast in this compound. I know that that idiot Jenkins has been talking to you about Lila. He has a fixation about her accident. Seems to blame himself, somehow. Ridiculous man. Refuses to face reality after twenty-five years.'

Her scorn for my friend angered me into an unwise course. I shot my question at her rapidly.

'Were Josh and Lila in love, Miss Miles?'

Now it was her turn to look startled, then furious.

'What a strange suggestion, Mrs. Trippe! The daughter of the household and the family groom? Unthinkable!'

'Why unthinkable? It's happened before. A beautiful young girl and a handsome, vigorous man with whom she spends hours sharing the same deep interest. Is that such an impossible situation?'

'For Lila and Josh Jenkins? Yes. An impossible situation. Lila may have been a bit of a flirt when she was very young, but I'm sure she always set her sights higher than a stableman.'

'On a doctor, perhaps?'

Milesy stood up. 'I have no idea what you're getting at, Mrs. Trippe. Nor, for that matter, why you are even here.'

'I'm sorry,' I said. 'I know I sound very curious. It's not that I mean to pry. It's just that I think there's a possibility that Lila might have suffered some shock that has made her an amnesiac. That's far different than brain damage, Miss Miles. I've seen both. I was a nurse, you know. There's a vast difference in the behavior of those who have irreparable damage and those who might respond to psychiatric care and maybe electric-shock treatments.' The stern, disapproving face made me flounder. 'It's only that I like her,' I said lamely, 'and from the little I've heard from Josh and Dr. Wiseman, I thought . . .'

The disapproval turned to rage. 'Your sources, Mrs. Trippe, are as unreliable as your diagnosis! You obviously don't have enough to occupy you that you can spend so much time speculating about things that are not only none of your affair, but have long ago been determined by highly qualified medical experts. I suggest you devote your time to your husband and leave his sister's well-being in the hands of those who've had many years' knowledge of her case!'

I jumped to my feet, offended by her rudeness. Still, it served me right. I was told not to interfere. Nonetheless, Milesy had no right to speak to me as though I were a meddling neighbor.

'Good-by, Miss Miles,' I said coldly. 'You need never worry about my troubling you again.'

Surprisingly, the woman looked ashamed.

'Please sit down, Mrs. Trippe,' she said. 'I'm sorry to have spoken as I did. It's only natural that you would want to help, but don't you see how terrible it would be if anyone *did* bring Lila back into the real world now? It would be torture for her. She'd know she'd missed the best twenty-five years of her life. I won't lie to you. When I first came here I, too, thought Lila might be helped. I even spoke to Mr. André about it, but he told me that the best neurosurgeons in the business were called in when Lila was injured. They examined her for weeks at the hospital back East. Miss Dolores saw to it all. I'm convinced now that they were right. And curing Lila after all this time, even if it were possible, would be cruelty. She's happy as she is. She's my little girl, and I won't let her be hurt. I'm sorry you came here, Mrs. Trippe. I was afraid that a young woman like you would stir up things at Madrugada. And you have.' She patted my hand. "Let's be friends,' she said. 'But no more talk of this. It's a closed chapter.'

I didn't know what to believe. Milesy's sudden transformation from an angry jailer to a pitiful woman who cared for Lila as though she were her own child took me off guard. I almost felt sorry for this middle-aged woman. And yet I didn't trust her, and no matter what she said, I could never be her friend.

All I wanted was to get out of this odd house, away from this strange woman who at one moment seemed steel-cold and at the next pathetically concerned for the protection of her charge. But protection against what? Why did they all feel that I was some kind of threat to the closed-in world they'd created?

'It's all right, Miss Miles,' I said. 'I won't interfere again. I'm sure you and Lila's family know best.'

I turned to leave but at that moment Lila appeared, smiling brightly, showing none of the fear she had on that first Sunday. Perhaps she was getting used to the sight of me. Or perhaps she only felt secure in her own home. At any rate, she approached me confidently, holding out her hand.

'You're . . . you're . . .' she searched for my name.

'Virginia,' Milesy prompted. 'You remember, dear. Roger's wife.'

Lila's smile broadened. 'Sure. Have you come to see me?'

I looked at the amazingly young face, the dark brown hair curling under in the old page-boy style, the cashmere sweater, skirt and saddle shoes, all a reincarnation of the '40s.

'Yes,' I said gently. 'I thought we might visit.'

'Super! Would you like to hear my records? Do you like Glenn Miller's "Moonlight Serenade"? It's my favorite. Shall I put it on for you?'

'That would be nice,' I said.

'And I'll fix us all a cup of tea,' Milesy said. 'Or perhaps you'd prefer coffee?'

It seemed an odd hour for tea, but Milesy was trying to make some show of hospitality.

'Tea will be fine,' I said. 'Thank you.'

The sweet, haunting sounds of the old song in the 'big band' style were beginning to fill the room. Halfway through the record, Lila began to dance alone. It was weird and sad to see her gliding around the room as though she were held in the arms of an imaginary or long-lost young man. When the record ended, Lila came and sat beside me, her big eyes fixed with interest on my face.

'I'm glad you came,' she said. 'Nobody ever comes. Did you like the music?'

'It's a lovely song,' I said. 'And you dance beautifully. You're very graceful.' I paused. 'Josh tells me you were a wonderful rider, too.'

Her eyes widened. 'Josh? Who's Josh?'

'He's that nice man in charge of the stable, Lila. We ride horses together every day. He says you used to love to ride. You had a little mare you named Virginia Dare. Don't you remember?'

Lila shook her head.

'Maybe you'd come riding with Josh and me one day,' I persisted. 'We could have fun.'

Milsey, entering the room with the tea tray, heard my last words. Her eyes flashed furiously at me, but her voice remained calm and cool.

'Lila doesn't ride,' she said, handing me a full cup of strong, black tea. 'She doesn't know the first thing about horses.'

This time I was determined not to lose my composure. I took a slow sip of my tea. It was sickeningly sweet but I pretended to enjoy it, saying nothing.

Lila's eyes over the rim of her cup looked troubled, as though something had rung a tiny bell, something vague and far away. She looked from Milesy to me and back again.

'Are you sure, Mom? I think maybe I used to ride. Maybe it was at school when you weren't there.'

'You're mistaken, Lila,' Milesy said. 'You've never been on a horse.'

A lightning change of mood came over Lila. Her voice became shrill and she banged her teacup into the saucer so angrily that the dark liquid spilled onto the rug. 'I have *so* been on a horse! Lots of times! I used to ride with . . . with Michael! Yes, that's it. Michael and I went riding all the time! Where is he? Where is Michael? Why hasn't he come to see me?'

Milesy moved nearer to the distraught woman. 'Darling, there's no one named Michael. Don't get yourself all upset. You know it's bad for you.' She tried to put her arms around Lila but was shoved roughly away.

'I want to see Michael!' The voice had risen to a scream. 'Why won't you let me see him? He brought me all my records. If you won't let him come here, I'll never let you listen to one of them again. Never, never!'

In a quick move she picked up the pile of old phonograph discs and sent then crashing to the stone hearth. They smashed into a hundred pieces. For a moment Lila looked at them uncomprehendingly. Then she began to shriek with frustration and rage, her cries finally turning into deep, anguished moans.

When Milesy looked at me I thought I had never seen such hatred. I was rooted to the chair, the empty teacup in my hand. I noticed, irrelevantly, that it was a different pattern than the others. The companion gathered a now unprotesting Lila into her arms and made little soothing noises. Then, over her shoulder she said, 'I think you'd better leave, Mrs. Trippe. And I'm sure you won't want to come back.'

'Is she all right?' I asked. 'Is there anything I can do?'

'You've done quite enough,' Milesy said bitterly.

'I'm sorry,' I stammered. 'I didn't mean to . . .'

'Of course you meant to.' The words were like slow drops of venom. 'From now on, please keep your little experiments to yourself. We don't need them here.'

She hurried the sobbing Lila out of the room. I let myself out and began to walk home slowly, trying to make sense out of it all. Had Lila recalled some part of her life in that brief moment. Was there really a Michael with whom she used to ride? I believed that there was. For a moment, at least, there had been some kind of lucid flashback. Did Milesy know that, or did she really think it was an aberration brought on by my probing? I was becoming more and more certain that Lila had amnesia and, peculiarly, that there was a determined effort to keep her in that state. But why? Why would the famly prefer she forget everthing that had happened in the last quarter of a century? And was Milesy part of the cover-up or simply a dupe, as much in the dark as the woman she cared for?

Halfway home I began to feel violently sick. My vision blurred and great waves of nausea swept over me. A few steps more and I knew that I was going to be actively ill before I reached my own house. I stepped off the road and retched hideously, dimly glad that no one could see me. The vomiting was so severe that it frightened me, and when it was over I lay helplessly on the grass, too weak to walk the rest of the way. It was a long while before I was able to stagger to my feet and slowly make my way to my own front door. I felt queasy but my vision had cleared and the sick feeling was slowly going away. Whatever it was, at least I had been able to get rid of it. Had I been married longer I might have suspected morning sickness, though I had never heard of it in such an acute form. And it was much too quickly dissipated to be a virus. I felt almost well now. It must have been something I'd eaten. But my breakfast was the usual juice, toast and coffee, The only unusual break in my routine was the cup of tea milesy had prepared. I remembered with a shudder its strange, over-sugared taste. She had not served it from a pot as I would have expected but had brought in cups already poured. And my cup was different. My God, had the woman tried to poison me? It was a ridiculous thought. But every symptom resembled poisoning. Not enough to kill me. More like a warning. More, I thought with horror, like the bullet that had come so close. That too could have been an attempt to frighten me into leaving Madrugada. If anyone had been aiming at me, he or she would not have missed. Dolores had said that everyone in the family was a good shot. I could hear her words now. 'Even Miss Miles can hit a tin can at two hundred yards.' Was this my second warning? Were both these threats from Miss Miles or from two different people? Or were they really no warning at all?

I tried to be rational. It could all have been coincidence. The stray bullet could have been just that. The bandana might easily have been there for months. Even this horrible, brief bout of illness could have been only a nervous reaction to the pathetic scene I had just witnessed at Lila's.

But I couldn't make myself believe any of that. Someone had tried to frighten me badly. Twice. Maybe there'd be a third time. Maybe next time they'd go beyond these signals and do the job somehow, somewhere, with finality.

I went to my bedroom, telling Rosita I didn't want lunch. After an afternoon rest I felt physically well. I had no fever, no symptoms of a virus. I almost wished

I had.

When Roger came home from the clinic I made him a drink and cuddled up close to him on the sofa. He stroked my hair absently and sighed.

'Gad, it's good to be home,' he said. 'The way they were lined up at the clinic today you'd have thought we were giving away free tricycles. What about you, love? Go riding?'

I hesitated, but I was not going to lie. 'You won't like it, but on the spur of the moment I went to visit Lila.'

He looked annoyed. 'Why?'

'I like her, Roger. I don't know why I shouldn't try to be her friend.'

He frowned. 'I don't think you ought to meddle in that situation, Ginny. Playing curbstone psychiatrist can be dangerous for the patient and for you.'

Instantly I was suspicious. 'What makes you think I was doing that? Playing psychiatrist, I mean.'

'Because Milesy called me at the clinic and asked me to keep you away. She said you disturbed Lila. Threw her into hysterics, in fact.'

'And you were waiting to see whether I was going to tell you,' I said slowly. 'You pretended you didn't know where I'd gone today.'

He didn't answer.

'Roger,' I said, 'what is this all about? Why is everybody so secretive about Lila, even you? She can be helped. I'm sure of it. But it seems that nobody wants her well. She remembered something today.

She remembered that she used to ride with somebody called Michael. Does that name mean anything to you, dear? It meant something to her. Some memory was trying to get through and she was frustrated at not being able to handle it. I know she could be brought back, Roger. I'm sure this is amnesia, not brain damage.'

Suddenly he was very angry. 'Textbook crap! Maybe she does remember somebody named Michael. How the hell would I know? And what does that mean, anyhow? She remembers Glenn Miller and Tommy Dorsey, but I doubt that she ever knew them! I want this nonsense stopped, Virginia. I mean it. Once and for all. My God, don't you think if Lila could have been helped my father would have gotten her the best care possible? He may be a tough old bastard, but he's not a fiend. She's his only daughter. Don't you think he'd want her memory restored if it was possible?'

I couldn't believe that this was my Roger. I was so shocked that my next words came out involuntarily.

'Yes,' I said, 'I think he'd want it restored – unless there was something he wanted her to forget!'

Roger stared at me darkly. 'And what is that supposed to mean? Do you think she murdered somebody? Or maybe she was guilty of some other dark evil deed – like cheating on an exam at that fancy finishing school. Virginia, you're becoming a terrible busybody. And that, combined with your active imagination, is bad news.'

'Please let me work at the clinic,' I said impulsively. 'I need to be busy and productive. I feel so useless. I'm not even the girl you married. I'll do anything, Roger. Run errands. Answer phones. I want to help people. I'm not used to being idle. That's the only reason I went to see Lila. And look at us. Saying ugly things to each other as a result of it. Please, sweetheart. Until we start a family let me work with you, even part time.'

He seemed to soften under my pleading, but although he took me in his arms and kissed me, his decision did not change.

'I'm sorry I was cross, darling,' he said. 'But the clinic is out. Wil told me you'd like to work there until you get pregnant. He thought it might be a good idea. But I don't. And neither does André.'

And neither, I thought silently, does Simon. I felt defeated and bewildered. Maybe, I told myself again, sheer boredom was driving me into fantasy. One thing was sure: I would not tell Roger about my sudden illness today nor, of course, about my lurking suspicions that my very life was in danger.

I didn't know what was happening to me. I felt friendless and frightened. Even my own husband seemed a stranger to me. And it was all based on nothing but strange, possibly unrelated events, and a terrible feeling that I should never have come to Madrugada.

Chapter Six

THOUGH NOTHING unusual happened in the next few weeks, the uneasy feeling that I was in danger from one or more people in the compound stayed with me. I tried not to let it affect my happiness with Roger who had returned to his gentle, loving self. But I was jumpy, suspicious of everyone, an attitude that was new and distasteful to me. Even my daily riding session did not hold the joy of those I'd had when I first arrived. I went daily to the stables and had become a proficient horsewoman, but the feeling of freedom and exhilaration was gone. I even told Josh that I'd decided not to call my horse 'Virginia Dare.' She would, I said without explanation, be called by her original name, 'Princess T.' He accepted my change of mind without comment but with, I imagined, a speculative, knowing look.

I prayed that I would become pregnant, believing that the arrival of a child would make me feel important and needed. But two months went by with no results and my depression deepened. I began to feel that even that happiness was to be denied me.

It was eerie that I saw none of the family except at the stilted Sunday dinners. I knew better than to go back to Lila's. Not only because of Roger's orders. I could not shake the frightening belief that Miss Miles really had tried to harm me. But it was odd that during that week I never saw Dolores, never caught a glimpse of the Senior Trippes or of Drew. Where did they stay all day? The Trippe estate was huge, but it was almost incredible that I would not catch sight of some of them as I roamed the grounds. I seemed to be the only one who ever used the pool, though it was kept in perfect condition. The tennis court, as far as I could tell, was never used except on two Sundays that Roger and I went over after dinner for a few fast sets.

I was twenty-four years old, healthy and convivial, used to a full life. But for two months I had lived almost like a recluse. I desperately missed the stimulation of other people and suggested to Roger that we invite some of his friends to dinner. But he pleaded that he was so harassed during the day that he wanted to be alone and quiet with me at night. Besides, he said, he really had lost touch with the few friends he'd had before he went East.

'Why don't we invite André and Dolores, then?' I asked. 'We could at least have "family." Maybe they'd bring Drew. I'd like to get to know them, Roger. It seems so strange that I never see even my in-laws.'

'We'll do that soon,' he promised. 'But André is as

beat these days as I am. And Dolores doesn't go out much. As for Drew, he has his own young friends, honey. I doubt that he'd want to spend much time with his parents and his aunt and uncle. You know how kids are. They like to be with their own.'

I was tempted to say that there was only a four-year difference between Drew and myself. It was not exactly like being asked to visit your ancient relatives. But I said nothing. Instinct told me I was living in the calm before the storm, as though something was going to happen that would disrupt all our lives. It was a weird, watchful feeling. I felt I was being observed by hidden eyes just waiting their chance to drive me away or drive me mad.

I did everything I could to occupy myself during the day. I spent hours in the stables, I gardened and even drove into the quiet little village a couple of days a week, taking Rosita with me to do the marketing rather than ordering by telephone as she usually did. But I was killing time, aimlessly making the hours pass and wondering always about the secretive, withdrawn inhabitants of Madrugada.

It seemed to me that the only one who sensed my uneasiness was Dolores. At the Sunday dinners she went out of her way to be kind, to make small talk with me. For the most part, the others ignored me. Lila refused to look in my direction and Miss Miles made no effort to hide her dislike. Drew was completely silent and the other Trippe men talked only among themselves. As for Natalie Trippe, she seemed to live in a perpetual state of nervousness, concerned only that nothing happened to displease Simon.

I tried to talk to Roger about it but found myself floundering. What could I say except that I was lonely? I could not say that I was afraid of his family. But that's really what it was. I dared not, despite Wil Wiseman's encouragement on that one evening, suggest to Roger that we leave Madrugada. He would think I was crazy. I had a beautiful house, a servant, a car, everthing I'd never had as an underpaid nurse from a modest family. How could I expect him to understand that I was like a lonely, hunted animal in a luxurious preserve? Sometimes I felt as though I was losing my mind. Reason told me that I had everything to be happy about. There had been no more near-accidents or unexplained illnesses. I had a devoted and adoring husband and all the creature comforts in the world. But I was lonely and still bewildered by the certainty that there was something important I didn't know. I knew that I represented some kind of threat. But what it was I could not imagine.

The first ray of understanding – or what I thought was understanding – came from my sister-in-law. Leaving the big house one Sunday, Dolores pulled me aside.

'We've all been very neglectful of you, Virginia,' she said. 'I'm sorry. It must be hard for you to adjust to the Trippes' solitary way of life.'

I could not deny it. 'It has been lonely during the day,' I said. 'But I'm now respectful of people's desire for privacy.' I gave a rueful little laugh. 'I'm sure you heard what happened when I barged in on Lila.'

'Yes,' she said quietly, 'I heard.' The beautiful face was full of compassion. 'You're so young,' she said. 'Too young for this kind of life.'

That's what Wil had said, I thought. Strange that the two people I felt I could relate to shared a concern about my ability to exist in this vacuum.

'Tell you what,' Dolores said suddenly, 'how about coming to me for lunch tomorrow?'

I was as pleased as if I'd been invited to a ball. I accepted eagerly.

'Good. About one o'clock?'

'Thank you. Thank you very much, Dolores. Don't go to any trouble, please. Just talking with another woman is going to be such a treat!' I smiled. 'I have Rosita, of course, but that's not exactly stimulating conversation. I've missed it. And I really want to get to know the family, especially you.'

I was being overly effusive, but I couldn't stop myself. Her casual invitation was like a friendly hand stretched out to someone drowning in confusion and self-pity.

'You *should* know the family,' she said. 'Though perhaps not especially me.'

Roger seemed mildly surprised when I told him about the invitation. 'You must have made quite a hit with Dolores,' he said. 'She seldom sees anyone.'

'Darling, I'm her sister-in-law! Why wouldn't she want to see me? I'd have thought we'd have become friends long ago.'

He shrugged. 'I told you before. She's a very private person, that's all.' He looked at me searchingly. 'Poor baby,' he said, 'you really are lonely, aren't you?'

I wanted to tell him everything I felt – the sense of displacement, even the fear, but now that Dolores had made a move toward me I hoped things might change. So I smiled. 'I'm like a house plant,' I said. 'They droop for a while when you move them to a new location. They need to be talked to and reasssured.'

'House plants are supposed to thrive on sunshine and love,' Roger said, 'and I've tried to supply you with plenty of both.'

'I know,' I said. 'And you watch. I'll begin to bloom again. Maybe I'll even be able to produce new leaves.'

An older version of Rosita opened the door for me next day. There was the same warm smile, the same attitude of genuine welcome. Ironic that I got on so well with the servants and the riding master and so miserably with the family. Unless you counted Wil Wiseman who had once been almost like family. I thought of him now, remembering that he had come to this house frequently in the past and wondering why he came no more.

Carmelita showed me into a charming, glass-enclosed porch that overflowed with plants and flowers sitting on the tile floor, standing on tables, hanging in rush baskets from the ceiling.

'The Señora thought you might enjoy lunching here instead of in the dining room,' she said. 'She'll be here immediately.' Carmelita paused. 'I thank you for being so patient with my niece, Señora. Rosita is a nice child but she has much to learn about keeping a house. She is very happy with you and Señor Roger.'

'We love her, Carmelita. And she's doing a wonderful job.'

The older woman looked grateful. 'I'm happy to hear that. Young people these days do not usually wish to go into domestic service. I was pleased that Rosita took to the idea. This is a good place to be, Señora. The family is kind.'

'You've been here a long while, haven't you?'

'Since Señor André and Señora Dolores were married. I was Rosita's age when I came.'

'Then you were here when they adopted Drew.'

Her expression changed. 'Yes, I was here,' she said. 'Please excuse me, Señora, I must see to lunch.'

The sudden, almost abrupt withdrawal surprised me until I realized that Carmelita probably thought I was becoming too personal. I had to remember that I was living in an old-world atmosphere where one did not chat easily with the staff. There were so many things I could not get used to here.

Dolores appeared at that moment and, to my pleasure, greeted me not with her usual cool handshake but with a little hug and a kiss on the cheek.

'I'm delighted to see you.' The voice was melodious

and almost loving. 'This visit is long overdue. My fault. But I promise we'll make up for it.'

'There's nothing I'd like more.'

She smiled. 'Tell me about you. Everything. Your parents. How you met Roger. The full story of – what is it – twenty-three years of life?'

'Twenty-four,' I said. 'Scary when you approach that quarter-century mark!'

She laughed. 'Not nearly as scary as when you're sneaking up on the half-century one as I am!'

I felt very much at ease as I launched into my life story. She listened carefully as I told her about my adoptive parents, my childhood and my work at the hospital where I fell in love with Roger. Even the quiet entrance of Carmelita with luncheon trays did not halt my monologue. Dolores seemed fascinated. She hung onto every word, not interrupting even to ask a question. It was as though she wanted to know every minute detail of my life. And I was so eager to talk that I went on endlessly, even confiding to her my life-long dream of finding my real parents.

'Not that Mom and Dad aren't wonderful,' I said. 'They've never been to California. I hope to get them here for a visit soon. You'll like them, Dolores. They're kind, gentle, outgoing people. They were so good to me, so full of love.'

'I know,' she said. 'Roger wrote so glowingly of the Barlows. He seems very fond of them.'

'They adore him,' I said, 'as I do.'

'Everyone loves Roger,' Dolores said. 'Not only

because he's a good man but I guess also because he's the baby of the family. There are almost thirteen years between him and Lila, you know.'

I wondered whether I dared ask the question that was uppermost in my mind. If there was a chance of anyone giving me a straight answer it was this understanding woman. I decided to risk it.

'Dolores, please tell me. What's the real truth about Lila? You were there when she had her accident. I have this strange feeling that there's more to it than the story I've been told. She remembers things. I found that out the other day. She remembered riding and someone called Michael. She got hysterical. I'm sure you heard about that. Please,' I said again, 'tell me what it's all about. It's not just idle curiosity. I really like her.'

For a moment I thought she was going to rebuff me the way Roger had or become angry as Miss Miles had. Or that she was going to stick to the story the way everyone, including Josh, did. Instead, she took a deep breath. Her face looked suddenly tortured as though she was torn between a desire to tell me the truth and a fear of doing so.

'All right,' she said finally, 'I'll tell you what happened. But I want your word, Virginia, not to repeat the story. You see, not even Roger knows the whole truth.'

'I promise,' I said.

Dolores fiddled nervously with the sleeve of her dress. It was the first time I'd ever seen her unsure of herself. Then she began to speak slowly, quietly.

'Lila and I were childhood friends. Our families were close, though the Trippes had all the money and power and my family had nothing but background. Enough to qualify us as acceptable to Simon, anyhow. When Lila was seventeen and I nineteen Simon sent her East to Miss Hawley's Finishing School in Virginia. Do you know it?' I nodded. It was a famous, exclusive place. 'I was already there, studying art,' Dolores went on. 'Lila arrived, presumably to complete her education. Instead, she told me that she had fallen in love with someone her father considered unsuitable, and Simon had quickly shipped her East to break up the romance.' Dolores smiled bitterly. 'I could understand that. You see, I, too, had been in love with someone, but Simon was determined that I'd marry André. The families had agreed to that, and I was too young and frightened to disobey them.

'But Lila was made of much sterner stuff. She had refused to tell Simon the name of the man she loved. But she told me. The man was Josh Jenkins.'

I sat utterly still. So I had been right about one thing. Josh had loved Lila. Still did, I was sure.

'Lila fully intended to defy her father and marry Josh. Not only because she loved him but because she was carrying his child. But nobody knew that part except me. She had, of course, not told Simon. And she had not even told Josh in the fear that he'd immediately go to her father and demand to marry her. Josh only knew that Lila loved him. He had no idea that she was pregnant. She had made Josh promise to keep the love affair a secret from Simon. It was her plan – which she had told no one – to get East, write Josh about his baby and have him join her there where they would marry and be beyond Simon's reach. But she never had a chance to do that.

'She did take a spill riding. It was a bad spill and it brought on a miscarriage in her fifth month. Lila wanted that baby so much that she had a nervous breakdown. I was the only one around, Virginia, and I was younger for my age than Lila. I never had her courage. I didn't know what to do, so I called Simon and told him the whole story. All, that is, except the name of the father. I knew Simon would kill Josh or that Josh would go out of his mind with remorse even if Simon simply did no more than send him away.

'My instructions from Simon were to do nothing. Just bring Lila home as soon as she could travel. He considered mental illness a disgrace, a blot on the family escutcheon. Not to mention pregnancy out of wedlock! So he put out the story about brain damage. The one that everyone has accepted.'

A tear rolled down her face. 'I know now that I should have been stronger. I should have insisted that Lila get psychiatric help, but I was frightened. It was unthinkable to me that I could stand up to Simon Trippe about the fate of his daughter. I wasn't even brave enough to refuse to marry his son.'

I went to her and put my arms around her. 'You mustn't blame yourself,' I said. 'You were too young for so much responsibility.'

Dolores dried her eyes. 'No,' she said, 'I was too weak to do what was right. Too selfish to pit Lila's future against Simon's wrath. I went along with it, Virginia, God help me, for months after the accident. I deprived that poor girl of the help she needed. And now it's too late. Too late for us all.'

'Maybe not,' I said. 'Maybe she could still be helped. Self-induced loss of memory can be corrected, even amnesia can disappear after years if it's treated.'

'No,' Dolores said again. 'You promised. You must not interfere in this, Virginia. You gave your word.' She looked frightened now. 'Swear to me that you'll not repeat this conversation. I can't tell you why, but it would be dangerous. Take my word for it.'

'All right,' I agreed reluctantly. 'I promise.'

Dolores sighed. 'Telling you makes me feel better. I've carried the burden of guilt so long. Do you hate me, Virginia?'

'Hate you? Of course not! I understand why you did what you thought you had to do. It must have been terrible for you all these years.' I did not mention the loveless match to André. That I could never understand. But my hatred for Simon Trippe was now stronger than ever. He had ruined four lives – Lila and Josh's, Dolores and the man she loved. And all for the sake of his precious pride, his tyrannical obsession to determine the destiny of those around him. I thought of Roger who admittedly had married me quickly before Simon could interfere. He knew that a child of unknown parentage would be anathema to Simon Trippe. I had known that from the first. Suddenly another question crossed my mind.

'Dolores, who is Michael? The man Lila mentioned.'

'The same man,' she said sadly. 'She hated the name Josh. She always called him by his middle name, Michael.'

'Poor Josh,' I said. 'Then he's stayed all these years just to be near Lila, even though she doesn't know him and he never can see her. He's an extraordinary man, isn't he?'

'Yes. Extraordinary. I've only known one other like him.'

She rose abruptly, once more the contained, composed Dolores that the world saw.

'I must let you go,' she said. 'And I must go, too. I have a thousand chores.' She kissed me lightly. 'Thank you for understanding, Virginia. Somehow I knew you would. And thank you for your promise. Swear you'll keep it.'

'I will,' I said. 'I swear on my mother's life.'

Chapter Seven

ALTHOUGH, OR perhaps because, I had given my word to Dolores that I would keep her secret, the tragic story was never far from my thoughts in the days that followed. The knowledge of that long-gone unhappy time made me sad and uneasy for the two young women involved and deepened my dislike and distrust of Simon. I could barely look at him on Sunday when we sat at the great, groaning dinner table. The idea of this unfeeling man dealing so dispassionately with others' lives made me almost ill, and I toyed with the enormous meal which was set before me, barely touching the inevitable salad which was the first course, pushing aside the succulent roast beef and potatoes which were the standard, hearty fare.

My listlessness and lack of appetite continued even at my own table. It was more than the lately acquired information, of course. I was bored with the sameness of my life at Madrugada and still edgy about the hostile attitude of some of the people who lived there.

Roger did not mention my obvious depression, but

he did not fail to take note of it. So much so , in fact, that he came home one evening and suggested that I join him on a short trip.

'There's a seminar in Boston I should attend,' he said. 'How would you like to go East with me, darling? It will only be a few days, but I thought perhaps while I was locked up in the meetings at Harvard you could run down to Washington and see your family.'

I leapt at the suggestion. 'Oh, Roger, *could* we? I would so love to see Mom and Dad! When would we go, and how long could we stay?'

It must have hurt him to see how eagerly I looked forward to getting away from his home and family, but he pretended not to notice my over-reaction.

'We'll leave next Monday,' he said. 'I'll go straight to Boston after I drop you off in Washington. You can have the week there and I'll come down on the weekend to pick you up.'

I was ecstatic. 'Let's call the folks right away!' I said. 'Thank you, darling! I'm so excited!'

He smiled. 'You'd think I was offering you the Grand Tour of Europe.' Then he sobered. 'Is it so awful for you here, Virginia? Are you sorry you married me?'

'Sweetheart, of course not!' I was suddenly filled with remorse. 'Marrying you is the most wonderful thing that ever happened to me! And it isn't awful for me here. It's just that I . . .' I stopped, uncertain how to put my feelings into words that would neither wound my husband nor reveal too much of the menacing atmosphere which seemed to be strangling me. 'I'm not used to country life, I guess. I miss the city and the activity. And, of course, I do miss my parents.'

'I know.' There was a wistful note in his voice. 'I wish mine could be replacements. "Madrugada,"' he said. '"Daybreak." There hasn't been much of a beautiful dawn for you here, has there?'

Now that I knew I was going to have even a temporary respite from the compound, I could sound genuinely cheerful.

'I've just been an old grump lately,' I said. 'I'm sorry, dearest. I truly am. I'll settle down. Just give me a little time to adjust.'

'You're not still worried about that stray shot, are you? You don't think it was aimed at you?'

I put on a good act. '*That?* Don't be silly! I'd almost forgotten it. My lord, that was the third day I was here! No, honestly, it's just the strangeness. It's such a totally different life. But you know what? I'll bet that after one look at the dirty, crowded streets of Washington I'll be dying to get back to the wide open spaces.'

He gently ruffled my hair. 'I hope so, darling. Anyway, the change will be good for you.'

Mother and Dad were waiting for us at the National Airport in Washington. I fell into their arms, crying with happiness at the sight of these two dear people.

'You look wonderful, baby,' my mother said. 'So tanned and healthy!'

'Even with mascara running down your face,' Dad said, laughing.

We had only a few minutes in the airport before Roger caught the shuttle to Boston. He kissed me fiercely before he boarded his plane.

'Have a good five days,' he said. 'And miss me.'

'I will, darling. You know I will.'

Though it had been only a few weeks since I'd left it, I'd almost forgotten how modest the Barlow house where I'd grown up really was. Compared to the vastness and grandeur of Madrugada, it seemed almost poor. But once inside, the warmth and familiarity of it cradled me with love. This was home as Madrugada could never be home, safe, undemanding and serene. My room was just as I'd left it, the souvenirs of my early years still intact. I wandered around touching the furniture affectionately, stopping to smile at a framed photograph of my high school graduating class, examining the nurse's diploma of which I was so proud.

From the doorway, Mother watched me silently, an anxious little frown wrinkling her brow. She knew me well. I never had been able to keep my true feelings from her, had never tried to in all the twenty-four wonderful years I'd lived with her.

'Want to talk about it?' she asked finally. She

seated herself in the armchair by the window while I curled up on my bed.

'Yes,' I said. 'I do.'

I told her everything that had happened to me, trying to keep the recitation calm, deliberately underplaying the threats I felt and underscoring the mutual love that existed between Roger and me. But I held back nothing. I even told her of my conversation with Dolores, something I had confided to no one else. It did not seem like a breach of faith to reveal what I knew to Mildred Barlow. It was a welcome relief to say aloud all the things that distressed and frightened me. Once put into words they became less ominous, far less significant than they had appeared when they were silent demons chasing through the troubled corridors of my mind.

Mother listened carefully, silently. I knew she was analyzing every word, weighing every disclosure, searching for a way to help me. When I finished, repeating firmly that I loved Roger and was happy with him, she went straight to the heart of the problem.

'You hate Simon Trippe, you dislike André, you don't trust them or Drew or any of the staff at Madrugada. But what's *really* troubling you is Dolores, isn't it? Her story has shocked you. Disillusioned you. I think you can't quite believe that a woman you like so much could have been so spineless as to follow Simon's orders about Lila and so frightened of him that she would marry his son whom she never loved. And I think,' Mildred Barlow added slowly, 'that you are convinced that in some way this is all tied back to you.'

I admired the clear, succinct way she had pinpointed the basic facts in my long, rambling story. She was right on all counts. But hearing it put this way made all my melodramatic interpretations seem hysterical and childish.

'You're an extraordinary woman, Mom,' I said. 'I wish I had your solid common sense.'

She brushed off the compliment. 'The important thing is, Virginia, what are you going to do about all this?'

I looked at her in astonishment. 'Do? What can I do except try to put it out of my mind. I have to accept the fact that Dolores is not quite the perfect human being I'd like her to be. I must tell myself what I know to be true – that I'm the luckiest person in the world to have a wonderful husband and a more than comfortable way of life. I'm going to devote myself to Roger and to the babies I hope to have, and let the rest of Madrugada go its own way.'

Mildred smiled. 'I wish it could be as easy as that for you. I know you, Virginia. You won't rest until you get at the bottom of these mysteries. There are doubts in your mind about Lila's illness and Dolores' account of the story. You're not the kind of girl who can close your mind to these things. Not while you have to live every day of your life with reminders of them.'

For a moment I was silent. 'But things that

happened to strangers twenty-five years ago really are no concern of mine.'

'You don't believe that.'

'No,' I admitted, 'I don't.'

Mildred got up briskly. 'Then why don't we use these five days to do a little detective work?'

I stared at her blankly.

'We can go to Miss Hawley's Finishing School. It still exists, not thirty minutes from here. Let's see what they remember about Dolores and Lila. And then,' the words came almost reluctantly, 'we can go to the adoption center where your father and I got you.'

'The adoption center! Why?'

'Because,' Mildred said, 'I believe that this morbid fascination of yours with Dolores and her adopted child and Lila and her unborn baby is magnified because of your own background. Maybe after all these years the agency will be willing to give us some clue about your own real parents.'

'You think there's a connection between Dolores' story and my own background?' I said slowly.

'I think no such thing. But since you were seven you've ached to know who you really are. It always hurt a little, Virginia, your yearning to find out, but as the years passed I thought you had almost forgotten your preoccupation with adoption. I can see now that Drew and Dolores and the rest have brought it into the forefront of your mind. If we're going on a fishing expedition about Dolores and Lila while you're here, we might as well lay those other ghosts to rest as well.'

My remorse was almost unbearable. How I must have wounded these two wonderful people with my constant wondering about my real mother and father.

'Even if I discovered who my parents were,' I said, 'they'd never be my parents. You're my mother and Daddy is my father. Nothing can change that.'

Mildred kissed me. 'I know that, darling. And so does Sam. And, frankly, I don't think we're going to discover anything more about your background at this late date. But you deserve the right to ask your own questions. Okay. Now get unpacked,' she said abruptly changing the subject. 'Your father is taking us out to dinner tonight.'

The next morning when Sam Barlow went off to work, Mother and I drove to Miss Hawley's Finishing School. Near as it was, I had never seen it, but I suspected that it had changed very little since the days of Lila and Dolores. It was a great mansion set among the trees. Beyond the main house I could see tennis courts and stables. Lila must have felt at home here, I thought. On a much smaller scale it was laid out similar to Madrugada, though the countryside was different and the great, white main house was architecturally more beautiful than the grim, gray home of the Senior Trippes.

There was a small office just inside the front door and a pleasant, plain-looking woman seated behind the desk.

'May I help you?' she asked cordially.

'We'd like to inquire about two of your former students,' I said. 'Dolores Del Cruz and Lila Trippe.'

The woman looked puzzled. 'I'm sorry. I don't remember ever hearing those names. When did they attend Miss Hawley's?'

'Around 1949 or 1950.' Suddenly I felt foolish. The receptionist must think us crazy, barging in and asking for schoolgirls who'd been here twenty-five years before. But if she thought we were mad, she didn't show it.

'I'm sorry,' she said again, 'but I'm afraid I must ask the nature of your inquiry.'

'They are my sisters-in-law,' I said. 'I'm Virginia Trippe. Married to Lila's brother Roger. And Dolores Del Cruz is now Dolores Trippe, married to Lila's other brother, André.'

The woman gave me a curious look.

'You see,' I lied,' 'I'd like to put together a twenty-five-year class reunion, a surprise for them. But I don't know the names of the girls who were here when they were. I thought perhaps I could look through the yearbook and perhaps contact some of them. And I'd like to talk to some of their teachers to get little anecdotes.'

I couldn't tell whether the woman believed my ridiculous story. In any case, she didn't bat an eye.

'Did your sisters-in-law graduate?'

'No,' I said reluctantly. 'I'm afraid not. But I thought perhaps I could get the names of girls who were their classmates.'

'That would not be possible, I'm afraid. We have yearbooks only of the graduating classes.'

'Then there might be someone here who knew them? Some teacher? Perhaps even Miss Hawley herself.'

'I fear not. Miss Hawley died ten years ago. Her niece runs the school now, but she was not here in 1950. For that matter, none of us was except Miss Thomas.'

I grasped eagerly at the one hope. 'May we speak to Miss Thomas? She might remember teaching Dolores and Lila.'

The woman behind the desk looked at me with distinct suspicion. 'Miss Thomas is not a teacher,' she said. 'She's a nurse. She runs the infirmary.'

Mother and I exchanged glances. All the better! If anyone would remember the details of Lila's accident it would be Miss Thomas.

Mother gave the receptionist a winning smile. 'It's not what we hoped for,' she said lightly, 'but would it be possible for us to chat with her? Virginia is so anxious to contact the other girls, but if she can't do that, at least she can make a little party for Dolores and Lila filled with some direct memories from a woman who knew them in their school days.'

The woman hesitated, but Mother's charm won her over.

'Well, there's no harm, I supose. The infirmary is just down the hall. Second door on the left. You'll find Miss Thomas there.'

We thanked her and hurried down the corridor. Well-groomed, obviously well-bred young girls hurried by us, their arms full of books. I tried to visualize Lila here. She would have looked then as she looked now, I thought. Or had she been a frightened girl, knowing she was carrying Josh's baby?

Miss Thomas greeted us cordially and listened calmly to our fabricated excuse for the visit. Then she went to her files.

'I'm afraid I can't give you much information of the kind that would help you with your party,' she said. 'The list of students for that year might be somewhere in the inactive files, but I wouldn't have it. I don't even have a folder on Dolores Del Cruz and not much of one on Lila Trippe. Neither of them was here very long, and apparently they were never ill. But I do remember them vaguely. Lila especially, because of that dreadful accident. She had a bad spill riding. A shocking thing. Of course we didn't attempt to treat her here. We called an ambulance and sent her immediately to Sibley Hospital. As I recall, her friend Dolores went with her.'

'But wasn't her family in contact with you?' I asked.

'Not directly with me,' Miss Thomas said. 'I'm sure they made all the arrangements with Miss Hawley. I did hear, I think, that Lila went to a private sanatorium for a while, but I have no idea which one.' The nurse shook her head. 'I remember her as a lovely child. I hope she's well?'

'Yes,' I said. 'She's fine. She and Dolores both.'

'I *am* sorry that no one here can give you any little personal memories of them,' Miss Thomas said kindly, 'but I'm sure you'll manage a lovely party all the same.'

We thanked her and left.

'Want to go back to the office and see whether they'll dig up the file of their classmates?' Mother asked.

I shook my head. 'No. Dolores' story must be true. It must have happened just as she said.' I frowned. 'We could look for information at Sibley Hospital, I suppose, but I'm not sure I need any more confirmation.'

'I'm afraid you couldn't get it very easily anyway,' Mother said. 'Don't you remember? They tore down the old Sibley a few years ago to make way for that new hospital complex.'

Our visit next day to the adoption center was even less productive, though a sympathetic man in charge deplored, 'off the record,' the existing practice of 'sealed records' in which the identities of the biological parents are kept secret unless the courts, for good reason, declare otherwise.

'I happen to feel,' he said, 'that upon reaching maturity every adult should have the right to know his background, see his birth certificate and the records of his adoption. There's a strong movement in existence right now – more than a thousand adults, adopted children, and legal and biological parents of adopted children – who're trying to change current legislation. But it's a tough problem. Highly emotional on all sides. Pity, if you ask me, that a person has to go through life with a never-ending identity crisis. But it's a touchy issue. Sometimes children have, on their own, discovered the identity of their real parents and have been appalled by what they found, or rejected by the people who gave birth to them. I don't know the answer. And I don't want to be quoted on this, if you please. But I can't tell you any more than you already know, Mrs. Trippe. Your natural mother had thirty days to change her mind after you were placed with the Barlows. From that time on she relinquished all rights to know anything about you.'

He would not, could not, budge on the matter of opening my files.

'Could my own parents have kept track of me?' I asked.

'Could have. Not legally, of course. It's considered as much an invasion of privacy on the life of the child to have its natural mother seek it out years later as it is an invasion on the privacy of the biological parents to tell the child at any point who *they* are. But some people have done it through private investigatory services. Maybe through guilt or just to assure themselves that the child they gave up is being well cared for by the adoptive parents.' He smiled at Mother. 'If Virginia's parents had kept track of her, Mrs. Barlow, I'm sure they'd be well satisfied.'

'But *she's* not,' Mother said. 'All she knows – all

that Mr. Barlow and I know – is that she was left with a baby ring and the name Virginia. That's very little to know about one's background.'

The man noded. 'I do agree, but not all experts do. Some believe that every child, adopted or not, goes through this identity search. Finding one's own parents doesn't necessarily solve it. The answer, like most things, lies within oneself. That's where *real* identity is.' He turned to me. 'I'm sorry, Mrs. Trippe. There's nothing I can do for you. Of course, if you want to pursue it, you could write to the Adoptees Liberty Movement Association, the group that's working for change. ALMA, it's known as. The Spanish word for "soul." I can give you their address here in Washington, if you like.'

'No,' I said, looking affectionately at Mildred Barlow. 'I think it's time I got rid of my adolescent daydreams. I have the best mother and father in the world.'

Mother was quiet as we got back in the car.

'Did you really mean that?' she asked finally. 'That very last thing you said?'

'About having the best parents in the world? You bet I did. I don't think I've ever realized it as fully as I have today.'

Mildred sighed. 'And now what, Virginia? We haven't found any answers. You don't know any more about Dolores and Lila than you did before you came. And you don't know any more about yourself.'

'Right on the first score, wrong on the second,' I

said. 'I know it's time I grew up. In lots of ways. I may never know who I am biologically, but I know who I am in my own right: your daughter, Roger's wife. The other things are not necessary for me to know. They're not even important any more. Distance does a lot for the perspective, Mom. I've been spinning a lot of self-involved daydreams for too long. I'm so absorbed with myself that I've even let my fears and distrust slosh over into my married life. Well, no more. Thank God for this trip. No more probing and poking,' I said. 'Not into my life or anybody else's.'

I truly meant it. All of it. I could see now that whatever happened to the Trippes long before I knew them was a part of their past, not mine. As for my 'biological' parents, I remembered what the man at the agency had said. Perhaps discovering their identity would be more disillusioning than the frustration of never knowing. Any girl would be hard put to find real parents more understanding and loving than the people who had cared for me all my life. As for Madrugada, if there were people there who didn't care for me, I'd have to learn to live with that. It was neurotic to expect everyone I met to like me. It was paranoid to interpret their dislike as a threat.

Satisfied, I put both matters out of my mind for the rest of my stay. It was a gay few days. I saw many of my old friends, visited the hospital where Roger and I had worked, shamelessly enjoyed the open envy of those to whom I described my new life, my home and housekeeper, my darling Princess T, my leisurely, unclouded days.

When Roger came to fetch me, I was genuinely happy not only to see him, but, I realized with pleasure, to be going back to my own home. It was the first time I'd thought of it that way and I was delighted to recognize how much I wanted to see my beautiful little house and the smiling Rosita. Mom and Dad promised to visit us soon. And I left content.

On the airplane I wound my arm through my husband's. I had told him nothing of my visit to the school or the adoption agency but he sensed that something had brought me a new inner peace.

'I was right, you know, darling,' I said. 'I *am* longing for the wide open spaces.'

He stroked my hand and smiled at me.

'You'll never know how glad I am to hear that,' he said.

I returned his smile. 'You'll never know how glad I am to say it.'

Our troubles are over, I thought contentedly. I can handle it all now, now that I've explored every avenue. How wise Mother had been to suggest that we do 'some detective work.' Fruitless as it was in all directions, it gave me an orderly sense of having tied off the loose ends of my life.

I had no way of knowing that the 'loose ends' were mere snips of problems compared to the tapestry of terror that would be woven around me in the days ahead.

Chapter Eight

A WEEK after my return I invited Dolores to lunch with me, but she begged off, saying she had a thousand things to do and asking for a 'raincheck' in the near future. Her voice, though cordial, seemed strained. I guessed that she regretted the unexpected burst of confidence and would avoid any more intimate conversation with me.

Strangely enough, a few days later I had an unexpected early morning visitor. Drew Trippe knocked on the door shortly after Roger had left for the clinic. It was a totally different Drew than the one I'd left. He seemed relaxed, friendly and appealingly boyish. Without the perpetual scowl he wore in his grandparents' presence, he was as beautiful as a young god. He lounged easily in my doorway, dressed in riding clothes, and smiling at my surprised expression.

'Welcome home,' he said. 'I know it's a shock, but I wondered if you'd let me ride with you this morning. I see you're dressed for it. Mind if I tag along?'

I was half-suspicious, half-pleased. What had brought on this sudden overture of friendship I couldn't imagine, unless he'd been waiting for some go-ahead signal. Perhaps my docile return established the fact that I was once and for all a member of the family.

'It's a lovely idea,' I said. 'I wasn't sure you rode. I thought skeet was your hobby.'

'Among others. I don't go to the stables much, but everybody in the Trippe family has compulsory riding lessons.'

'Like compulsory shooting lessons?'

'Yes,' he said. 'It's part of being a Trippe.' He gave me a half-smile. 'When are *you* going to learn to handle a gun?'

'Never.'

We were walking toward the stables now, Drew swatting at bushes along the road with the riding crop he held. We were silent for a long while, only the soft crunch of our boots breaking the morning stillness. It was a beautiful, warm day with a clear blue sky punctuated with great soft clouds like globs of shaving cream on the face of the universe. I felt strangely happy. It was good to have young companionship; as good as it was unexpected. It was even good to be back at Madrugada.

'Where do you keep yourself every day?' I asked, idly.

Drew shrugged. 'Just around.'

'I've hoped to see you,' I said companionably, 'but

you're never visible except on Sunday.'

'I go into town a lot,' he said. 'What's to hang around here for?'

I had to agree, though I didn't say so. Certainly there was no diversion for a twenty-year-old on summer vacation. I knew that he went to college and Roger had mentioned that Drew was planning to enter medical school, but the summers must seem endless to him in this lonely place.

'I hear you're going to follow in your father's footsteps,' I said.

'My father's? You mean André's, I suppose. He isn't really my father you know. I'm adopted.'

'Yes, I know. So am I. We have something in common. A lot, in fact. We were both blessed with wonderful adoptive parents.'

He gave me a strange, cynical look. 'I guess I'll be a doctor,' he said. 'That's what *they* want.'

'Isn't it what *you* want?'

'Does that matter?' For a moment he was the scowling young man who sat beside me at dinner. Then, abruptly, his mood changed again. The frown disappeared as we entered the paddock area. 'It really is something, isn't it?' he said enthusiastically. 'I forgot how damned impressive it is. Look at it all. My God, it's like being a Whitney or a Vanderbilt, being part of this. And some day it'll be mine.' He stopped short as though he'd just thought of something. 'No, it really won't be mine, will it? If you and Roger have children it will be theirs, won't it? I mean, they'll be honest-to-God Trippes. Not adopted bastards, like me.'

'It seems to me you're getting awfully far ahead of yourself,' I said. 'Roger and I haven't even started a family yet.'

'But you plan to.'

'Well, yes, of course, we hope to. But not for the purposes of inheritance, I assure you.'

He hesitated as though there was something he wanted to say and then apparently thought better of it.

'Don't be in a rush,' he said.

He strode briskly ahead of me before I had a chance to ask what he meant. By the time I caught up with him he was already talking to Josh who had ordered Princess T and two other horses saddled. Josh greeted me warmly.

'How about this young fella?' he said. 'First time I've seen him around here in weeks. Might have known it would take a pretty girl to bring him out where he belongs. This guy's a helluva rider, Virginia, but he doesn't seem to care much about it.' Josh grinned. 'Maybe just as well, at that. When he brings one of the horses back to the stables I have to give her a rest cure for a week!'

Drew laughed. 'Work hard, play hard and always be best. Isn't that Simon's motto, Josh? What do you want me to do, canter along like some old lady?'

'No. I'd just like you not to break your damned-fool neck or kill one of your grandfather's horses.' Behind

Drew's back, Josh shook his head at me as though to say he's a reckless kid and I won't let you ride alone with him.

The three of us mounted and began a leisurely canter down the path that I took so often with Josh. Drew was in the lead, maintaining a brisk but sensible pace that I, directly behind him, was able to follow. Josh brought up the rear as we proceeded along the peaceful, tree-lined way. We had been riding for perhaps five minutes, when Drew pulled his horse to the side and I came abreast of him.

'Just to show Josh that I can be a good boy,' he said, 'you take the lead, Virginia. That way I won't get too far ahead of you. I know you're a beginner at this.'

Josh was beside us now. 'Don't worry about Virginia,' he said. 'She can hold her own with the best of us. She's the best horsewoman I've seen since your Aunt Lila used to ride before you were born.'

'Is she, now?' Drew's eyes narrowed. 'Well, then, maybe I should challenge her to a race. How about it, Virginia?' He pointed to some distant woods. 'A dollar says you can't beat me to that tallest tree down there. And I'll give you a head start.'

'Forget it,' Josh said. 'This is a pleasure outing, not a competition.'

'No, it's okay,' I said. 'I don't mind losing to Drew.'

'Maybe you won't lose,' Drew answered.

I dug my heels into Princess T and took off at a gallop, Drew starting a few seconds later. The hot wind tore at my face as I urged the little mare on, faster and faster down the winding path. Once or twice I looked back over my shoulder. Drew was steadily gaining on me, a determined look on his face. Josh was making no effort to keep up. He was falling far behind, almost as though he had no desire to be part of the performance.

'Come on, baby!' I said. 'Let's show him!'

Princess responded with increased speed. I had never ridden so fast and I felt frightened even as I pressed harder. I was not a good enough rider, in spite of Josh's compliments, for this kind of race. And still I urged Princess on. My hat flew off and I had to duck occasionally to avoid low-hanging limbs that came upon us almost before I had time to see them. I bent low over Princess, fiercely determined to win, breathing hard now, not daring to look back at Drew. There was no need to. I could hear the pounding of his horse's hooves gaining steadily on me. A few more minutes and he was beside me. There was barely room on the path for the two of us. And then, incredibly, as Drew passed me he gave Princess a sharp, stinging blow with his crop. She reared up on her hind legs, startled by the unexpected attack. I held on with all my might, trying to bring her under control, frantic in my efforts not to be thrown. Miraculously, I stayed on her and finally brought her to a stop. I was shaking and limp when Josh reached me. Drew was almost out of sight, riding heedlessly, hell-bent for the destination we had set.

'Virginia, what happened!' Josh's face was full of

concern. 'What made Princess rear up like that? What frightened her?'

'Drew,' I gasped. 'He hit her as he passed me.'

Josh looked puzzled. 'Hit her? Hit your horse? What in God's name would make him do a thing like that?'

My composure was slowly returning. 'I don't know,' I said slowly. But I did know. He wanted me to fall. To be badly hurt, maybe even killed. Was it Drew who threatened me? Had he been the one who fired the warning shot weeks ago? It was perfectly possible. But it was not Drew who had put something in my tea. Or was it? Could he somehow be in league with Milesy?

I felt as though I was going to be sick again, but this time I knew the cause. In all my life I'd never felt endangered by another human being. And now everyone was suspect. Even Josh. Why had he stayed so far behind? Did he know what Drew planned and was careful not to be a witness? Dear God, I said, don't let Josh be part of this conspiracy, whatever it is. Not this gentle man whom I had grown to love and trust.

'I can't believe Drew meant to frighten Princess,' he was saying now. 'Why would he do such a thing? Good Lord, Virginia, you could have been killed! It must have been an accident. He probably just got excited and hit Princess instead of his own horse, by mistake. He's a wild, headstrong kid, but he'd never do something like this intentionally.'

'Wouldn't he?' I asked sadly. 'I'm not sure what anyone here would do.'

Josh's bewilderment seemed real. I wheeled my horse and rode slowly back to the stables, Josh following silently. A few minutes after I dismounted, Drew came racing in, his horse covered with sweat from the inhumanly hard run.

'What happened?' Drew said. 'What made you stop, Virginia? When I got to the tree I saw you and Josh turning back.'

'Drew, did you hit Princess when you passed her?' Josh's voice was stern.

'Hit her? Why would I hit her?'

'You did, Drew,' I said. 'You deliberately frightened her and she reared up. I didn't think I could stay on.'

He looked at me incredulously. 'Are you crazy? Why would I try to frighten your horse? Hell, I had you beat by a mile.'

The two men looked at me. 'He's right, Virginia,' Josh said. 'He was passing you easily. I could see that even though I wasn't in the race. Princess probably shied at something she saw on the path. Maybe an animal or a piece of cloth.'

I didn't answer. But the words 'a piece of cloth' made me realize, for the first time, that both men were wearing red bandanas with a small T in the corner. Wordlessly I walked away from them. It was possible that because Josh did not try to keep up he didn't see Drew hit my horse. But the boy knew very well what he had done. And it was no accident.

'I owe you a dollar, Drew,' I said coldly. 'I'll give it to you next time I see you.'

'Virginia, wait!' Drew came running after me. 'I swear I didn't hit Princess.'

I just looked at him.

'If I did, I have no memory of it,' he said. 'So help me God, that's the truth. I was riding hard. That I admit. But if my whip hit your horse it was unintentional. If it happened, I meant to hit my own.'

'Don't insult me with such nonsense, Drew. You did it on purpose. You know you did.'

'No! Honest to God! If I did such a crazy thing, I didn't even know I was doing it. But I couldn't have. I just couldn't have.'

He seemed genuinely distraught and remorseful.

I looked at him curiously. 'Are you telling me that you do things you don't remember? Come on, Drew. You must be able to think up a better excuse than that.'

He kept his eyes on the path, walking slowly beside me. 'I don't know,' he said in a low voice. 'Sometimes Mother tells me I've said or done something that I honestly don't remember. And at school I fainted a couple of times. Just blacked out.'

My nurse's instinct came to the fore. 'Have you told anybody about this? Have you told your parents?'

He shook his head.

'What about school when it happened? Didn't they take you to the infirmary for examination?'

'It happened in my room in the dorm. Nobody saw.'

I was becoming alarmed. 'Drew, you must tell your father about this loss of memory, these fainting spells. You should be examined. If you won't talk to your father, then discuss it with Roger. Or with Wil Wiseman.'

At my last words he became violently angry. 'No! Not with any of them. Especially not with that bastard Wiseman. He's the last one *either* of us should talk to!'

'But, Drew,' I protested, 'if what you tell me is true, you're sick. You need help. Look what happened a few minutes ago. And you say you have no memory of it.'

He underwent a sudden, violent reversal. 'Nothing happened. It was like Josh said. Something in the path scared Princess. Why don't you stay the hell out of everybody's business, Virginia? Isn't one loony in this family enough for you?'

I turned scarlet. 'I don't need that talk from you. And I know what I know, Drew. In spite of anything you can say.'

'You don't know anything,' he said roughly. 'And you never will.'

I watched him disappear rapidly down the road. For a moment I let him go. Then I ran after him.

'Drew! Come back!'

He stopped and waited for me.

'Look,' I said, 'maybe I did imagine it. I was terribly excited and scared while we were racing. Let's forget it. We'll forget everything that has been said today.

Come back to the house for lunch. We both need to settle down after all this.'

He looked at me suspiciously with the old hostile expression.

'Why the sudden change of heart?'

I tried to laugh. 'You and Josh must be right about that little incident. As for the other stuff, it could happen easily from fatigue, overwork. Probably you were pushing yourself too hard at school. Anyway, Drew, I do want to be friends. I truly do.'

I waited to see whether he would accept this explanation. None of it was true. But I sensed that Drew was my best, maybe my only hope of unraveling the mysteries that surrounded me. Even if he was the one who'd been menacing me, I was certain that only through this strange boy could I get at the heart of the riddle.

He considered my words for a long moment. Then he seemed pacified. 'Okay. I guess we both got a little excited.'

'Sure we did. Come on. Rosita will feed us.'

Whether Drew was telling the truth about his lapses of memory I could not be sure. It could as easily be that he was lying for some purpose of his own. Or even that he was being used as a tool by someone intent on getting rid of me. I didn't know which way to turn. Normally, I would have confided in Roger, but he'd seemed so impatient with me when I'd told him about the first episode that I hesitated to mention the things that followed. For that matter, Roger seemed unusually preoccupied these days. It was as though the withdrawn attitude of the Trippe family had reached the younger son now that he was home again. Home. I had no home here. Only a house. The happiness I'd felt on my return was gone again. Wil Wiseman had encouraged me to try to get Roger to leave the compound. I knew that only a miracle would make him even consider such a thing. He seemed perfectly content with our way of life. But then, he had his work and his contact with the outside world. I had only this abandoned, threatened feeling, day after day.

Even the friendship with Drew – an idea on which I'd once concentrated – had brought me added uneasiness which I tried hard to dispel. The boy had become a regular visitor to our house now. I saw no more of the strange, brooding quality in him. He was a cheerful companion these days. We swam together and played tennis. We spoke no more of his troubled mind. Nor, by tacit agreement, did we ride together again. And there were no more inexplicable 'accidents' in the weeks that followed the horse race. But I was never completely relaxed in Drew's presence.

By early August, however, I had almost persuaded myself that the Trippes had grudgingly accepted me. Dolores and I exchanged no visits and thus never pursued our earlier conversation. But at least we were friendly when we met weekly at the main house.

Sometimes I caught her looking at me oddly, almost wistfully. But she offered no explanation and I dared not ask for one. Even André and Simon seemed less resentful of my presence at the Sunday dinners, and Natalie had become almost timidly affectionate. Drew, as noted, was almost a constant companion. Only Lila and Milesy acted as though I did not belong in the family. Lila seemed afraid of me, influenced, no doubt, by her companion who made no secret of her violent dislike.

And then, one deceptively peaceful summer day, something happened that drove me close to the edge of madness.

Drew and I had been swimming and were sunning ourselves at the pool, making small talk. I was, in fact, telling him that I seriously thinking of taking up painting as a hobby.

'Not that I'd probably be any good at it,' I said, 'but I used to dabble in oils when I was at high school.' I did not say that I searched feverishly these days for anything to keep me occupied. 'I thought it might be fun to take a crack at it. We have a number of your mother's paintings at the house. Maybe that's what's inspired me. She's very good, isn't she?'

'I guess she used to be,' Drew said. 'It was all before my time. I don't think she's painted in years. But there must be a hundred canvases stacked up in that little cottage back of our house.'

'Really?' I was interested. 'I'd love to see them, but I know the studio is kept locked. Rosita says that

Carmelita doesn't even go there to clean.' Then I realized what Drew had said. 'How do you know there are paintings there? I thought no one was allowed in.'

'They're not. I jimmied a window a couple of years ago.' His face took on a strange expression. 'I had a hunch there was something in the place that Dolores didn't want anybody to see. Why else would she put it off limits?'

I tried to keep my voice casual. 'And you found nothing but a bunch of old canvases, right?' I laughed. 'What were you looking for Drew? Hidden treasure?'

'In a way. I was looking for the same thing you've been looking for. Some clue about my real parents.'

'And you expected to find it in the studio?'

'Maybe. It would be a good place to keep adoption papers or correspondence, wouldn't it?'

'I suppose so,' I answered. 'Provided they weren't safely tucked away in some safe deposit box. That would seem far safer and more logical to me for people like André and Dolores. Anyway,' I was baiting him now, 'I'll bet you didn't find anything.'

His face flushed. For a minute he was the wild-eyed young man at the stables, offering me a dare. 'You know better than to bet with me, Virginia. Remember the last time? I only bet on sure things.'

'Okay,' I said casually. 'Bet's off. Forget it.'

'Would you like to see what I found?'

'Not particularly.'

As I guessed it would, my feigned indifference spurred him on. He pulled me to my feet. 'Come on.

I'll prove it to you. We'll go in through the window. I'll show you what's there.'

I hesitated. I was curious to see the studio, intrigued by what Drew thought he had discovered. But I was also reluctant to be alone with this unpredictable boy in a cottage that no one ever came near.

As though he read my mind, Drew smiled. 'What's the matter, Virginia. Scared to be alone with me?'

'Don't be ridiculous. It's just that it's trespassing, Drew. I don't think it's the right thing for us to do.'

'You're scared,' he taunted. 'You're afraid we'll get caught breaking in.'

I tried to laugh. 'Well, I've never fancied myself in the role of a second-story man, that's true.'

'Come on.' It was no longer a request, it was an order.

Reluctantly I put on my slacks and moccasins. I did want to see what was inside the studio but instinct told me that I might get more than I bargained for. If Drew really meant me harm, I was giving him the perfect opportunity. A deserted house, set off by itself. A place no one had entered for years. He could kill me and leave me there and God knows when anybody would find me.

Nonsense, I told myself. Drew might be erratic, even possibly a little unbalanced, but he wasn't going to murder me in his mother's studio. Without another word I followed him to the cottage and climbed in after him through the window.

Chapter Nine

THE STUDIO was not at all what I'd expected. There was an easel beside a north window and canvases, dozens of them, lined up against the wall. But it was more a little home than an artist's workshop. There was a bedroom, kitchen and bath, in addition to the living room. And though dust lay thick on everything, the charm and cosiness of the house reached out to me. It was comfortably, invitingly furnished, the kind of place one might picture as a lover's retreat, a hideaway for very private people.

Drew watched me intently as I took it all in.

'But it's charming!' I said. 'Why on earth has Dolores closed it off? If it were mine, I think I'd want to spend hours here. It's so restful and' – I searched for the right words – 'so *personal*.'

'Notice anything odd about it?'

I looked around. 'Odd? No, I don't think so. What do you mean?'

He pointed. 'Look at the photographs on that wall.'

I followed the direction of his finger. One whole

wall of the cottage was covered with pictures of Dolores, Drew and Wil Wiseman. I went closer for a better look. There were photographs of Dolores with Drew and Wil with Drew and snaps of each of them singly. There was no picture of the three of them together. And there was no sign of any other familiar face in this strange gallery.

'What does it mean?'

'That what I wondered when I first saw it,' Drew said. 'Why does my mother have pictures of Wil Wiseman all over the wall of a locked studio? And why, if the three of us are the idols of this shrine, are we never photographed as a group?' He lit a cigarette and lounged back against the wall. 'Answers: The pictures are there because I'm the illegitimate child of Dolores Trippe and Wil Wiseman. And we're never photographed together because no one could be trusted to take a group picture. There are none of the two of them together because a baby can't snap a camera at his parents.'

I stared at him. 'Are you trying to tell me that based on some old photographs you've concluded that Wil is your father and Dolores your real mother? Drew, you're crazy! There's no way!'

'There's every way. They were in love before she went off to school. She came back, married André but continued the affair with Wil. This is where they used to meet. What Victorian novels called their "trysting place." André knew he was sterile, so when Dolores miraculously became pregnant a couple of years after their marriage he must have sent her away to have the baby, and then they pretended to adopt a strange child.'

'That's the wildest fantasy I ever heard! Listen, Drew, it doesn't make sense. Not from any angle. If André knew about the affair with Wil Wiseman, he'd have divorced Dolores, not adopted her child!'

Drew shook his head. 'Simon Trippe doesn't believe in divorce. And André is Papa's obedient little boy. He'd do as he was told.'

'But what about Dolores and Wil? Why didn't they claim their child? And how could André and Wil go on working together knowing about this?'

Drew shrugged. 'Who knows what makes people tick? My theory is that Dolores was too frightened of the Trippes to do anything. As for Wil, he's a no-good bastard who'd put his career ahead of anything. It probably pleased him to know what André was thinking every time he looked at him. André couldn't bust up the partnership with Wil without blowing the whole story wide open. All André could do was take out his anger on my mother and me. Which he has, for twenty years.'

I was stunned. I didn't believe the picture of Wil that Drew had painted. I liked him, trusted him. As for Dolores, it was impossible to believe that she was so timid that she allowed this intricate 'face saving' plot. Yet she'd admitted to me that she'd loved someone else and given him up under pressure. That person could have been Wil. I could see how she could love him and even continue to see him after her loveless marriage to André.

'You still don't believe me, do you?' Drew asked. He reached deep into a bureau drawer and pulled out a thick old scrapbook. 'Take a look at these old letters in the front of the book. And then tell me again that I'm crazy.'

Reluctantly I read the first letter. It was undated but the paper was yellow with age.

'Dolores, my darling,' it said. 'I cannot condone what's been decided about the baby, but I force myself to recognize the necessity for the course you've made up your mind to follow. God, I shouldn't say "made up your mind"! It has been made up *for* you, hasn't it, my dearest, my beloved, beautiful angel? I try to understand the reasons for what you're doing, just as I try to live with the knowledge that I can never claim *you*. I try to be grateful for what I can – your love and the blessed fact that you will soon be home again. I was afraid, at first, that the pregnancy might be terminated. This way, at least, is less heart breaking. We will always know that the child is alive and well. That, hopefully, will assuage some of the sorrow. You are brave and wonderful. I love you and only you, now and forever. Wil.'

There were tears in my eyes when I looked up.

'There are others,' Drew said. 'Lots more gutless protestations of love from my hypocritical father while my mother was away having his child. Go on, Virginia. Read them.'

I shook my head. 'No. I feel as though I am prying into someone's soul. God, those poor people! I don't believe Wil Wiseman is a hypocrite, Drew. I think he had no choice. Dolores was too intimidated to do anything but what she did. And probably too guilty about her unfaithfulness, even to a husband she didn't love. The one I can't understand is André. How could he live with a woman who didn't love him, with a child who was hers but not his? How could he work with a man who'd been his wife's lover and fathered her baby?'

'If nothing else, he'd do it out of revenge,' Drew said. 'There isn't an ounce of humanity in André Trippe. And I told you, he's Simon's shadow, Simon's slave. If he couldn't have children of his own, at least he could see to it that there was a boy to carry on the precious family name.' Drew laughed mirthlessly. 'If I'd been a girl, they probably would have drowned me.'

I remembered Wil's surprising denunciation of André the one and only time we'd talked. I understood it now. Just as I understood that Dolores' guilt about Lila was intermingled with guilt about her own secret. I sighed. The photographs were not proof of Drew's theory, but the letter was. A full and open admission of Wil's intimacy with the woman I liked so much.

Idly, I flipped to the later pages of the book. There were pictures of all the family, carefully marked. Snaps of André getting his college degree, older ones of Simon and Natalie taken in front of their house. And then, suddenly, a picture of a beautiful little girl perhaps two or three years old. Under it, Dolores has written, 'Lila on her third birthday.' I looked at it carefully. She was overdressed in a frilly frock and hair ribbons. But what caught my eye was her left hand. On it was a baby ring. Not just any ring. An exact duplicate of the one I'd received on my seventh birthday. The one that lay in my jewelry box now. The one Roger had roughly forbidden me to wear.

It seemed an eternity, though it probably was only a few seconds, that I stood staring at the picture. I was certain that it was my ring. True, the photograph did not show color, and there might have been any number of rings like it. I had even seen one or two in antique shops. Not quite the same, but similar in design. 'Friendship rings' they were called in Victorian times. Each stone represented a letter – an emerald for 'e,' a diamond for 'd' – so that the band spelled a word like 'dearest' – in diamond, emerald, amethyst, ruby, emerald, sapphire and tourmaline. In my mind, I saw the little band that was now in my bureau drawer, but it seemed to make no sense: emerald, peridot, pearl, ivory, ruby and turquoise. It made no sense. 'Eppirt.' Unless, I had been looking at it backwards for seventeen years! Read from left to right, the stones spelled a different word. 'Trippe.'

I tried to absorb what it meant. I had Lila's baby ring; left by a mother who had demanded that I be named Virginia, and Virginia was Lila's favorite name – the one she had given the filly she adored. I could easily accept the latter fact as coincidence, but what was I doing with Lila's ring? Who had left it with the adoption agency three thousand miles away?

I rubbed my hand over my eyes. Forgotten now was Drew's amazing theory about his own parentage. I was barely aware of the cottage, the photographs on the wall, the impassioned letter from Wil Wiseman to Dolores. All my consciousness was fastened on this new and bewildering discovery that was connected to me . . . and the things that happened to me since the day I came to Madrugada.

Drew stood watching me, saying nothing, a curious look in his eyes. Had he meant me to find the picture? Was everything else a ruse to get me to turn to that particular page in the scrapbook? But why? Drew had never seen my ring. No one in the family except Roger had. I felt like a trapped animal. Where did the explanation lie? Why did I own the baby ring that had belonged to my husband's sister? A hundred thoughts flashed through my mind, but uppermost was the most unthinkable of all: the horrifying idea that I was Lila Trippe's child – with all that that implied.

I could not hide my distress any more than I could explain it. I turned to Drew.

'Could I . . . that is, would it be all right if I borrowed this photograph?'

He came across the room and looked at it.

'The baby picture of Aunt Lila? What do you want with that old thing?'

'I like it,' I lied. 'It's charming. I thought maybe I could copy it in a painting.'

He didn't believe me, of course. I was much too agitated. But he simply made an uncaring gesture.

'Sure. Why not? Nobody ever looks at this old book. But if anybody sees the painting, for God's sake don't say what you copied it from.'

'I won't,' I promised.

My hands trembled as I tried to remove the old photograph which had been glued tightly onto the page. I fumbled, terrified that I'd rip it as I tried to pry it loose. Drew took the book away from me.

'Here,' he said, 'let me. You're going to tear it to pieces.'

Slowly, gently, he separated the picture and handed it to me intact, the sticky glue leaving marks on the conspicuously empty space in the book.

'Thank you.' I slipped the photograph into the pocket of my slacks. 'I'll return it after I'm through with it.'

'Funny you picked that,' Drew said. 'Funny, but not surprising.'

I was instantly alert. 'Why funny? Or not surprising?'

He looked innocent. 'I don't know. It's just a dumb old snapshot. Funny you'd like it. But not surprising because you're so hung up on kids.'

I didn't answer.

'Maybe you're upset that you're not pregnant yet,' Drew suggested. 'You don't think Roger has André's trouble, do you? I mean, sterility doesn't strike twice in the same family does it?'

'How dare you?' I was angry. 'What utter gall to be so personal, Drew!'

He was all charm again. 'I'm sorry, Virginia. I didn't mean to pry. Anyway, maybe it's just as well that you're not having a baby.'

What was he trying to tell me? 'I don't know what you're talking about.'

'Nothing. That is, I just meant this is a hell of a place to bring up a kid. Ask me. I know.'

It seemed wiser to let the matter drop. I didn't want to hear any more about Drew's own – or fancied – background. All I wanted was to get home and compare the picture with my ring. To make sure that my mind really wasn't going. More than once in the past few weeks I'd had reason to doubt my sanity.

We climbed back out the window, Drew closing it tightly behind us. On the way back to my house, he made only one more reference to the secret visit and the things I'd found there.

'Quite a family tree we've been grafted onto, isn't it? A skeleton hanging on every branch.'

I tried to smile. 'Don't turn it into a Greek tragedy, Drew. After all, at least you have your real mother.'

'Sure. Even if she pretends not to be.' He gave me a jaunty salute in farewell. 'That's more than you can say, isn't it?'

I rushed upstairs and took the little ring out of my jewel case, comparing it closely with the dim photo. I hadn't imagined it. I owned the baby ring that Lila had worn.

For the next few tortured days I kept my secret and my suspicions to myself. There was only one person who might be able to tell me anything – Dolores. But I could not show her the evidence without disclosing the fact that I had been an intruder in her studio. For that matter, there was no one in the family to whom I could show the picture without revealing the fact that I had shamelessly pawed through private possessions to which I had no right of access. I wondered how Dolores had dared hang the revealing pictures of herself and Wil on the cottage wall. How could she be sure that André wouldn't take it into his head to go into the little house? But then, of course, André knew about her and Wil. The pictures might anger him but they'd be no more than a minor irritation compared to the full story which, according to Drew, he already knew.

The scrapbook was a much deeper secret, I was sure. It had been buried in a drawer, I remembered now. Even André, had he decided to go into the studio, would very likely not have spent time going through all its contents as Drew had. And even if someone in the family remembered the ring, no one except Roger knew that I now owned it.

So I could not show the picture to anyone but I could, pretending innocence, show my ring to someone. Perhaps I would get an involuntary reaction, even if I ran the risk of arousing suspicion that I was trying to piece together a forbidden story. Dolores, though she was the logical one, was also the most intelligent. She would wonder why I suddenly produced my only link with the past. No, it had to be someone naïve and basically kind. Someone who had known Lila all her life and who loved her. The choice was simple. I had to talk to my mother-in-law.

It took me nearly a week to get up enough courage to approach her. I felt guilty not telling Roger about my mysterious development, but I justified my secrecy by convincing myself, through long sleepless nights, that he was too young to know about jewelry that had belonged to a girl who was a teen-ager when he was born. Simon would know, of course. And André. But it was patently clear that I could not talk with either of the men whom I felt were my enemies.

It had to be Natalie. I lay awake beside my loving, unsuspecting husband, wondering what pretext I could use to talk to her. I decided it would be better to get Natalie to my own house if I could. She and Simon had never been there. Roger had made it clear that his parents never visited the other residences in the compound, seldom left their own quarters, in fact. But I didn't want to have my hoped-for conversation in Natalie's home. Simon or Mrs. Angus could always appear unexpectedly and put an end to whatever revelation I might be about to uncover.

As it turned out, luck was with me. On the Sunday preceding my invitation to Natalie, we inadvertently arrived at the main house a little early. My mother-in-law was not yet in her formal, 'hostess pose.' She was seated in a little sitting room adjoining the main salon, holding an exquisite piece of needlepoint. Roger went off to find Simon and I timidly went into the little room where Natalie was intently working on an intricate design. She jumped when she saw me, embarrassed that she was not ready to receive her family.

'Oh, my dear!' she said. 'Forgive me. I was so involved that I completely forgot the time!'

'We're a little early,' I said. 'I think our clocks have gone haywire.' I looked at the work in her lap. 'What a beautiful piece,' I said. 'My mother does the same kind of exquisite needlepoint.'

'Really?' Natalie seemed genuinely interested. 'And do you like to do it too?'

I laughed. 'Unfortunately, I'm all thumbs. But Mother just sent me some marvelous things, including a magnificent rug for our bedroom. It took her years to make it.'

'A courageous undertaking,' Natalie said. I'd never seen her so relaxed. 'I've never attempted anything more than pillows or chair seats.'

'I'd love you to see it,' I said quickly. 'Would you come tomorrow? For lunch, perhaps?'

I held my breath. God had dumped the perfect opportunity in my lap. I couldn't lug the great rug which had, indeed, arrived only a few days earlier, to the main house for Natalie to see. My mother-in-law hesitated.

'Luncheon? At your house? Tomorrow? Oh, I'm afraid not, my dear. You see, I never dine out.' Then, perhaps because I looked so crestfallen, or more likely because she was eager to see the needlepoint, she suddenly relented. She lowered her voice conspiratorially. 'But,' she said, 'if you were to be at home about three o'clock tomorrow afternoon, perhaps I could drop in for a few minutes. Mr. Trippe has to drive into town for a business meeting and Mrs. Angus always rests at that hour.'

'Three will be perfect,' I said. 'I'm so eager to have you see our house.'

'The needlepoint rug,' she said. 'That's what I most want to see.'

'Of course.'

She rose. 'The others are arriving, so we must go in.' She looked worried. 'You won't say anything about our little plan? Mr. Trippe doesn't think I'm well enough to go out, and Mrs. Angus follows his orders.'

'It will be our secret,' I promised.

She patted my cheek. 'You're a nice child.' There was a wistful note in her voice. 'You could be my granddaughter, you know. I'm getting so very old.'

The words, so innocuous, brought back the feeling of the sinister atmosphere of this house in which Natalie Trippe was a prisoner. Worse, they brought me closer to an insane idea that had not left me since the day in the cottage. What if I really were Natalie Trippe's granddaughter?

Chapter Ten

IN SPITE of my pact with Natalie Trippe, I did tell one other person that I expected a visit from my mother-in-law. Rosita had to know, since she would be in the house when the lady arrived. If, I thought, she *did* arrive. I was not sure that Natalie would even remember the appointment, much less keep it.

My housekeeper reacted with surprise when I told her that Señora Trippe was coming to call. Her astonishment was so great that she momentarily dropped her role as the almost-invisible, deferential servant. Indeed, she seemed overly agitated by the news.

'Here?' she asked incredulously. 'Señora Trippe is coming here? But she goes nowhere! Carmelita says that she never leaves her own house. Dr. André takes care of her needs. He goes every day to give her the injections . . .' Rosita clapped her hand over her mouth.

'Injections? What injections?'

Rosita seemed frightened. 'I don't know, Señora. I

should not have mentioned it. Carmelita will kill me.'

I was puzzled. 'Does Mrs. Trippe have diabetes? Does Dr. André give her insulin? Is that it?'

The girl retreated into silence. It would have been cruel to press her. It must be diabetes, I thought. That was why she was so carefully watched, so sheltered from anything that might upset her and worsen her condition. But my medical knowledge refuted the simple explanation. I had watched Natalie at the table. She ate everything, including the richest, sweetest desserts. Besides, diabetics did not live as invalids. There was no need to shut the woman off from the world if she had something as easily controllable as a disease that could be handled with proper doses of insulin. If Natalie Trippe was getting daily medication, it was for some other reason.

'It's good that she has a doctor right here,' I said offhandedly. 'Diabetics sometimes find it difficult to inject themselves.'

Rosita seemed to relax. 'Yes, it is a difficult thing. I know I could not do it to myself or anyone else. Carmelita is much stronger. Dr. André has taught her how to plunge in the needle. She can tend to Señora Trippe when Dr. André is too busy to go.'

I pretended to dismiss the subject. 'We must be sure that everything is nice for the Señora when she arrives,' I said. 'She wants to see the needlepoint rug my mother sent me, the one that came a few days ago.' I weighed my words carefully. 'I don't plan to tell anyone that she's coming to visit us. We wouldn't want to offend Señora Dolores or Señorita Lila by letting them know that she's made an exception for us, so let's not mention it, all right? I won't tell Dr. Roger, and I don't think you should say anything, not even to Carmelita. No use upsetting the family, is there?'

'No, Señora. I swear. Not a word.'

I felt that Rosita would keep her promise, not only out of loyalty to me but, more practically, because Carmelita would worm the whole conversation out of her and be angry that she had told me about the mysterious injections.

I dressed carefully for my mother-in-law's hoped-for call. As though it were Sunday, I exchanged my usual casual clothes for a cotton dress. And as a last, deliberate touch, I fastened the gold chain with the baby ring around my throat, not hiding it as I always had, but letting it glitter conspicuously against the white linen bodice.

A few minutes past three, the door knocker rapped sharply. I ran to open it and found myself staring not into the gentle eyes of Natalie Trippe but into the angry face of her husband.

Simon brushed past me into the foyer. Clenched fists on hips, strong little body thrust aggressively forward, he faced me threateningly.

'Just what do you think you're doing?' he demanded.

I faltered. 'I don't understand what you mean.'

Simon's face was flushed. 'What is this cock-and-bull story about a needlepoint rug? Why are you trying to talk to Mrs. Trippe alone?'

The shock which had almost left me speechless was beginning to wear off. 'It's no cock-and-bull story, Mr. Trippe. Your wife said she'd like to see the rug and I was happy to invite her to see it. Besides,' I said, emboldened, 'is there some strange California law that says a woman isn't allowed to visit with her mother-in-law? Or is it that you're afraid Mrs. Trippe will say something you don't want known if she's out of sight of you or Mrs. Angus?'

For a moment I thought he was going to strike me. Then, unexpectedly, he began to laugh, an indulgent condescending laugh that made me feel like a melodramatic fool.

'Let's sit down, Virginia,' he said. 'I think we have a few things to straighten out.'

Obediently, as though it were his house, I followed him into the living room. Simon lounged easily in a big chair, looking at me with amusement.

'Are you a big reader of detective stories?' he asked. I didn't answer. 'You must be,' Simon went on. 'Since the day Roger brought you here you've been building up a fantasy about Madrugada and the Trippes. Oh, I know it all,' he said. 'A stray shot that you believe was aimed at you. A chance bandana of which there are hundreds. A cup of tea that you think was laced with poison. A horse that bolted. Even,' he said grimly, 'unlawful breaking and entering, an offense for which I could have you jailed.'

I was open-mouthed with astonishment.

'Nothing that goes on at Madrugada escapes me, young woman. Nothing. Your every act, almost your every thought is brought to my attention. This is my world, my empire. I don't like it disturbed with your hysterical fancies and your imagined signs of evil. I won't have my daughter-in-law questioned about the past, my daughter upset by your probing and my wife spirited away by you, for whatever reason, to be disturbed by more of your ridiculous suspicions.'

There was no trace of amusement on his face now.

'I want you to forget your insane fantasies now,' he said slowly. 'I want no more disruption. There was none of this nonsense at Madrugada before you came. There will be none in the future.'

Involuntarily I grasped the little ring at my breast.

'Are you threatening me, Mr. Trippe?'

He smiled. An unpleasant smile. 'There,' he said. 'Typical. Even a friendly piece of advice, designed only for your well-being and that of your new family, is interpreted by you as something sinister. Tell me, Virginia, is there any history of insanity in your family?'

I flushed. 'You know as well as I do, Mr. Trippe, that I don't know anything about my family.' I paused and then said boldly, 'But I thought perhaps you did.'

For a moment I thought I had taken him off guard, but I could not be sure that my words meant anything to him.

'I know only that I was not in favor of my son's

marriage to a girl whose past is unknown. But he made his choice, hastily but irrevocably, until death do you part. I accept that. As I expect you to accept the way of life here. No one is trying to harm you. I don't know what motivates your strange behavior and your theatrical and sometimes underhanded actions, but I know that all this nonsense must cease. Including your secret attempts to visit with my wife who, as I'm sure you've guessed, is not well and who is not coming today or ever.'

He rose. 'You've caused me to miss an important business engagement,' he said coldly. 'Try in future not to inconvenience me.'

He started for the door. Impulsively I grabbed the sinewy arm.

'Will you answer two questions for me?'

He shook me off impatiently.

'Please,' I said, 'if you do, I promise not to bother you again.'

He paused. 'What are your questions?'

'Is Mrs. Trippe physically ill? If I knew what kind of shots she gets every day maybe I could help. I'm a registered nurse, you know.'

Simon smiled sardonically. 'So *you* have a grapevine working, too. You know about her medication. Interesting. All right. Mrs. Trippe gets Vitamin-B shots. As simple as that. Since she does not like sunshine and fresh air, André has prescribed them for years. What is your second question?'

I held out the little ring. 'Have you ever seen this

before?'

He looked at it closely without a flicker of expression 'No. Should I have?'

I couldn't answer without giving away the secret of the photograph. Simon knew, somehow, that I had been in the cottage but it was unlikely that he knew I had gone through the secret scrapbook, or even that one existed. There were some things, I thought with satisfaction, that even the Señor didn't know. I was sure he recognized the ring, that he was lying about never having seen it. But it was possible that he knew nothing of any link to me. He was a good actor. But he couldn't recite lines that he didn't know had been written.

Without another word he left my house, slamming the door decisively behind him. As I turned away I caught a glimpse of Rosita disappearing into the kitchen area. With dismay I knew she had been listening to every word.

Upset by the encounter, I changed into my swim suit and robe and walked slowly to the pool. As I passed the main house there was no sign of life. As usual, the shades were drawn and the great, gray pile of rock seemed lifeless. I wondered how Simon had found out about Natalie's proposed visit. There had been no one around when we spoke. Probably she had told him about wanting to see my rug, not realizing, in that vague way of hers, that Simon would know she'd have to come to me. But how had he found out about the appointed hour? It was understandable that he'd known about the bullet. Roger and everyone had known. And he could have heard about the horse incident from Josh. But I had told no one about my violent illness after the visit to Lila. And I couldn't believe that Drew would have confided in Simon about out secret trip to the studio.

Most of all, why did Simon deny ever having seen Lila's ring? He remembered every detail of family history, and the little jeweled band must have been an heirloom. I had put it away again when I changed, but it stayed in mind, a tantalizing clue to my past. Lying at the pool, my fears mounted. If the ring was Lila's then only she could have left it for me. Could she have had a baby and given it for adoption, not miscarried as Dolores had said? Was the guilt of separation from her child the reason for Lila's self-induced amnesia and the whole riding accident story invented by Simon to cover up the existence of an illegitimate child? Had Dolores lied to me? My knees turned to water at the prospect of the twisted truth, for it would mean that by a mad stroke of coincidence, Roger had married his own niece. I turned away from the thought with horror. There had to be some other explanation for this dreadful, incestuous possibility! God could not be so cruel as to play such a monstrous trick on me and the man I loved.

But I knew, with unbearable sadness, that until I found the answer I dared not be a wife to the man I married. And I was too frightened to tell him why.

The next days and nights were like a bad dream. I longed to go to Dolores and tell her the whole story, beg her to tell me the truth and explain how I had come into the possession of a ring worn by Lila. But I could not betray Drew, and I dreaded the words I did not want to hear. At night I pleaded fatigue and bad headaches to a bewildered Roger who was understandably puzzled by my withdrawal from him. After a week of this, my husband became genuinely concerned.

'I don't like the way you're feeling,' he said one night. 'There must be something physically wrong. Unless you don't love me any more.'

My heart ached, but I would not risk even putting my arms around him.

'You know I love you,' I said. 'More than anything in the world.'

'Then what is it, darling? You've been deliberately avoiding me. Is something upsetting you? Can't we talk about it?'

I longed to tell him everything, all the secrets I had been keeping from him. I yearned to be reassured that I was not Lila's child and that the peculiar incidents I'd encountered were pure chance. I wanted to believe Simon, that this was all a web of circumstantial evidence, adding up to nothing. Even the ring could have been a similar one with six stones. There was no proof in the black and white portrait that the jewels were the same. But reason could not overcome my panic. I could never rest until I got at the truth.

Roger was waiting for my answer.

'Nothing is upsetting me,' I lied. 'I just haven't felt well. I'll get over it.'

'That's a strange attitude for a woman who knows a lot about medicine,' he said. 'I think we'd better arrange for a thorough check-up. I'll set it up at the clinic.'

For the first time I smiled. 'At the clinic? Darling, I may be behaving childishly, but I'm not a pediatric patient. Besides, I honestly don't want a check-up with André, and you obviously can't do it.'

'No, but Wil can. He's a first-rate internist as well as pediatrician. And he's not in the family.'

Reluctantly I agreed. There was no way around it, even though I knew my physical heath to be good. In any case, it would give me what I most needed – time.

I was surprised the next afternoon to receive a telephone call from Dolores. She had avoided me for weeks, and though she was pleasant enough when we met on Sundays, she gave no indication of taking the 'raincheck' I'd offered on my return.

'Virginia, dear, I hear you're not feeling well.' The voice registered genuine concern. 'Is there anything I can do?'

André, I assumed, had told her about my impending visit to the clinic. There were no secrets in this family, I thought ironically, except the ones that were kept from me. Not that it mattered in this case.

'I've just been a little off my feed,' I said. 'Nothing serious. Roger's more worried than I. But it's nice of you to offer.' I paused. 'How have *you* been, Dolores?'

The implication did not escape her. She laughed apologetically. 'You must be annoyed with me for not having gotten back to you about lunch. I've meant to.' She sounded suddenly serious. 'I've had a lot on my mind, I'm afraid. Drew's been behaving so strangely. I'll be glad when the summer's over and he goes back to college. It's so boring for him here. I know he misses being with people his own age. Lately he's taken to driving off in the morning and not returning until very late at night. I don't know where he goes or whom he sees.'

It occurred to me that I had not seen Drew alone since the day we broke into his mother's studio. I thought of Lila's photograph hidden in a locked suitcase in my bedroom closet, and I remembered the boy's anger as he told me what he knew of his parentage. Perhaps, like Dolores, he regretted having let me in on his secret.

I groped for a way to ask Dolores about the ring in the photograph, but of course there was no way. I could not believe that she had lied to me about Lila's miscarriage and her own part in the deception but there was no way to make sure. Instead, I tried to reassure her about Drew.

'I wouldn't worry too much,' I said in answer to her last remark. 'Drew can take care of himself. Maybe he has a girl in town.'

'Probably you're right.' The voice belied the words.

'I keep forgetting that he's really a man. I still see him as that little bundle we were handed twenty years ago.'

Drew's version of how Dolores received 'that little bundle' echoed in my ears. He *had* to be the one who was not telling the truth. And yet there were all those photographs on the wall of the cottage, and the letter that spoke with such concern about 'the baby.'

We hung up, I promising to let her know the results of my examination and she swearing that we would get together within the next few days.

'I do want to see you, Virginia. You must believe that.'

'Of course,' I said. 'I know how time gets away.'

I did know. It had been a while since I'd been near the stables. Since the day, in fact, that Princess T and I had had our bad scare. That event had added to my distrust of everyone, even Josh. He had taken Drew's side, had gone along with the boy's version of what had – or had not – happened. I was still angry with him for that, and yet I was sad too. Josh had seemed my one friend in the beginning. It was hard to believe that he had joined the conspiracy of hatred that seemed to surround me.

Conspiracy of hatred! The sound of it inside my head shocked me. What an overly dramatic creature I had become! It was myself I should be angry with. All this speculation and suspicion was building to a point where I saw deceit in everyone. I had to stop it, before it possessed me. After the check-up I would wipe out the memories of imagined horrors and try, once again, to become the happy, uncomplicated bride who had arrived at Madrugada.

The idea made me feel better. I knew well how the mind can magnify the most insignificant detail, how even the least important word or action can assume the proportions of terror without the control of a disciplined mind. I had always prided myself on my common sense. All I had to do was coldly examine things that had terrified me. Viewed objectively they would be meaningless, individual coincidences that I had contorted into an overblown plot.

Almost cheerful for the first time in weeks, I put on riding clothes and walked briskly to the stables. Josh was unabashedly delighted to see me.

'Well, it's about time!' he said when I walked into the tack room. 'Thought maybe that little scare had put you off riding altogether. Figured you'd turned chicken on us.'

The gruffness did not disguise his relief nor his pleasure at my appearance.

'I was scared out of my wits,' I admitted, 'but that isn't what's kept me away. We were on a trip, and since we've been home I've been busy.'

'Good,' He gave me that warm, twinkling smile that had always made me feel so close to him. 'The Princess has been asking for you. Going to take a little ride?'

'Maybe just a short work-out in the ring.' I said. 'It's late in the day and besides you look too busy to go with me,'

He sighed. 'End of the month accounts. Mr. Simon's pretty fussy about them. It's the only part of the job I hate.'

'Josh,' I said idly, 'haven't you ever thought of moving on? You must have had offers all these years from really big stables. I'll bet you could have trained a triple-crown winner.'

'Oh, sure, I've had offers. From some of the best. But this is home, Virginia. Everything I love is here.'

There was no emotion, no hint of hidden meaning in the simple words. He was just a plain man without great ambitions. So much, I thought, for my romanticizing about Josh and his lost love.

It was good to be back on Princess T, cantering briskly around the ring, feeling the strong muscles of the little horse's body beneath me. I patted her lovingly and imagined that she was as glad to see me as I was to see her. We had been exercising for about half an hour when Josh came running out of the stables.

'Virginia! Come quickly! Mrs. Angus is on the telephone. Something has happened to Mrs. Trippe!'

I hurried to the phone. Mrs. Angus sounded frightened. 'Can you come at once? I don't know what's wrong with the Señora. She's unconscious. I can't rouse her!'

'Have you called André and Roger?'

'Yes. They're on the way, but I thought maybe in the meantime . . .'

'Yes, of course, I'll be there in a few minutes.'

I hung up. 'Drive me to the main house, will you, Josh? It sounds serious.'

I found the formidable Mrs. Angus helpless with fright. Natalie Trippe lay apparently lifeless across her bed, her breathing shallow and her pulse slow.

'What happened?'

'I don't know,' the housekeeper said. 'Dr. André was busy so Carmelita came and gave Mrs. Trippe her shot about an hour ago. A little while later when I looked in on her she was unconscious. I couldn't rouse her. I called the doctors, but I thought maybe you could do something until they arrive.'

'Put more pillows under her head. It might help her breathing.' Natalie seemed to be struggling for every breath. 'And get brandy. She looks like she's having a heart attack.' I kept my fingers on Natalie's pulse. 'Where is Mr. Trippe?'

'He went out before Carmelita came,' Mrs. Angus said. 'I don't know where he is.'

Josh was standing quietly in the background. 'Can I do anything?' he asked. 'Maybe I should call for an ambulance.'

'No, I'm sure André and Roger will be here any minute. They'll know what to do.'

I watched Natalie closely. The brandy which Mrs. Angus forced down the slack mouth seemed to have no effect. Knowing nothing about her condition, I did not know what to do for her. It could be a heart attack, a diabetic coma or half a dozen other things. The worst thing I could do would be to take some uninformed action. I prayed hard, waiting to hear a car arrive. It was no more than ten minutes, though it seemed an eternity, before Natalie's sons burst into the room.

Heedless of us all, they rushed to her side. André examined her quickly. 'Call an ambulance,' he ordered Roger.

'I'll do it,' Josh said. 'You stay with your mother.'

I touched Roger's arm. 'What is it? What's wrong with her?'

It was not Roger but André who answered.

'Overdose,' he said. 'Goddamn that Carmelita!'

In that instant I noticed that Roger looked as shocked as I. Overdose. Natalie Trippe was on hard drugs.

Chapter Eleven

GUILTY THOUGH it made me feel, Natalie Trippe's grave illness brought welcome escape from my sequestered life at Madrugada. She was rushed to the hospital in Los Angeles, and I learned that the daily injections were not mysterious. They were, indeed, drugs, but painkillers to ease the poor woman's agony against the cancer that was slowly destroying her.

Peculiarly, until Carmelita had accidentally administered the overdose, no one but André and Simon had been told the seriousness of Natalie's disease. The shock I'd seen on Roger's face was real. Even he had not known that his mother was dying, and his grief at the knowledge was so deep that I reached out to him with love and comfort as I had when we first married. I closed my mind to any consequences, any possible wrongness of resuming my marital relations with my husband. He needed the strength and forgetfulness that only I could give him. The wrong – if there was wrong – had already been done. He clung to me desperately and I returned his desire, determined to forget, at this awful moment, the suspicions I still entertained.

For the next few weeks I drove into Los Angeles almost every day to visit Natalie. It was a relief to get away. Sad though the journeys were, it was the first time I'd been outside the compound on a regular basis. Except for my one early visit to the clinic and the quick trip East, I'd been virtually a prisoner on the Trippe estate. Sometimes Dolores or Mrs. Angus went into the city with me. But for the most part I made the drive alone, pleased to be free. After the few minutes I was allowed with the patient, I spent the rest of the time driving around Bel Air, the rich residential section, or browsing through the stores and boutiques that infested Wilshire Boulevard and the affluent area of Beverly Hills. I even allowed myself the luxury of buying new 'California clothes.' The ones I had brought from the East were, I realized, an Easterner's idea of a West Coast wardrobe. They were too classic, too severe for this casual world. Unconsciously, I imitated the things I'd seen Dolores wear, the flowing palazzo pajamas she'd worn when we lunched, the easy dresses she appeared in on Sundays, the clinging silk shirts and impeccably tailored slacks she put on for the trips to Los Angeles. My own understated wardrobe contained too much black and white, beige and gray. I indulged myself in bright but not flamboyant pants suits and in simple little 'Sunday dinner dresses' of clinging jersey in sharp, clear colors, a far cry from the subdued 'city linens' I had bought for my trousseau.

I justified the frivolity of a shopping spree with the knowledge that Natalie's disease was momentarily arrested. We were no longer maintaining a death-bed watch, though we knew that all we could do was buy the greatest asset of medicine – time. Roger insisted that it was not necessary for me to visit Natalie so often, but I continued to do so, hating myself for the knowledge that escaping Madrugada was as strong a motive as going to see my mother-in-law. The Freeway didn't frighten me. I enjoyed driving. And, because of my background, the hospital atmosphere did not hold the horror for me that it did for those unfamiliar with the sterile surroundings. I found the brisk efficiency of the nurses comforting, the matter-of-factness of the staff familiar and reassuring. And though she was weak and uncommunicative, Natalie seemed glad to see me. I felt closer to her in that period than I ever had before. Even Simon, to my great surprise, told me that he appreciated my attentiveness. One Sunday in a strange change from his usually hostile attitude, he thanked me for my visits.

'Mrs. Trippe looks forward to your coming,' he said. 'You seem to give her more reassurance than the rest of us.'

The words, offered with difficulty, made me soften toward Simon. He really loves her, I thought. Remembering his last visit to my house I knew now that he was trying to keep the serious nature of her illness a secret, determined to protect his sick wife from the strain that my own agitation might have put on her. Sensing that he would have been embarrassed by a response I simply smiled my thanks, a smile I hoped would also indicate that I would not upset Natalie in the future. Simon seemed to understand. In a rare gesture of affection he patted my cheek and then turned brusquely away from me, never to mention the matter again.

After a series of cobalt treatments at the hospital, Natalie came home and my excuses for visits to town ended. Things returned to the way they were when I first came to Madrugada. With Natalie's improvement, each member of the family became engrossed in his own preoccupations and I was once again left to my own thoughts and the resumption of my anxieties.

At Roger's insistence, a date for a thorough physical was scheduled with Wil Wiseman. I knew perfectly well that there was nothing organically wrong with me, but I could think of no valid excuse to avoid the check-up. Now that his shock and sadness had abated, Roger no longer had the urgent need to which I had determined to respond. I began to turn away from him again, beset by the lurking suspicions that had been temporarily and deliberately set aside. I felt strange about undergoing a physical with Wil. I had seen more of him these past weeks. We sometimes ran into each other at the hospital when he came to see Natalie and once or twice we'd had lunch together in town when our visits coincided.

I found him a fascinating older man, and though he was always polite and proper he made no secret of his obvious affection for me. Although we discussed nothing of importance over lunch, I felt drawn to Wil, almost too personally involved to let him be my doctor. I considered telling Roger that I'd rather have my check-up done by a stranger, but if my husband asked me – as he would – why I didn't want Wil, I had no logical answer. I could hardly say to Roger that there was some mysterious bond between Wil and me. It would have inferred a physical attraction that, on my part, at least, did not exist. I concluded once again that I was being foolish. Wiseman's fondness for me was warm and friendly, nothing more. It was the same kind of easy affection he'd projected on the one and only night he visited Roger and me. Perhaps I was seeing him in a new light because of what Drew had told me and because of the incriminating evidence of Wil's affair with Dolores which I'd found in the studio. In any case, it did not concern me. If he had loved Dolores, if, perhaps, he loved her still, it was no business of mine. And it certainly had nothing to do with a doctor-patient relationship between the two of us.

Since the discovery of the baby picture of Lila I had perversely resumed wearing the baby ring on a thin chain around my neck, never taking it off, even to bathe. Roger noticed but did not comment, nor did I offer any defense or explanation. My link with the past had become part of me again and I almost forgot it was there under my clothes, invisible to all but those who saw me in a swim suit or a nightgown. Only Roger saw the latter and no one the former. Drew no longer sought me out at the pool and apparently no other member of the family who was at home during the day shared my passion for the sun and water.

So familiar had the ornament become to me that I forgot to remove it when I undressed and wrapped a sheet around me for my check-up in Wil's section of the clinic. He came into the room when I was ready for the examination, greeted me coolly and professionally and began to take my blood pressure. It was then that I saw his gaze go to my throat where the baby ring dangled from its chain. I imagined I saw a flicker of surprise in the dark, intent eyes, a little jolt of recognition, gone in a split second. He said nothing but that tiny moment confirmed my suspicions. It *was* Lila's ring I was wearing and somehow Wil knew that it was. Deliberately I put my hand to my throat.

'I forgot I was wearing this,' I said. 'Shall I take it off for the chest X ray?'

His expression didn't change. 'Might as well,' he said matter-of-factly. 'It could throw a shadow.'

I unfastened the tiny clasp and put the jewelry on a towel-covered table beside me.

'Don't let me forget it, Wil. It was my mother's.'

My gentle prodding didn't shake him. He was the impersonal doctor with the stethoscope on my back, ordering me to breathe in and out, listening intently. I looked at the little ring as I obediently inhaled and exhaled. It glittered in the sunlight and once again I silently repeated: turquoise, ruby, ivory, pearl, peridot, emerald. Trippe. It seemed to be sending me a message. 'I am the key that unlocks your parentage,' it said. 'Are you so afraid to use me, Virginia?'

Yes, I answered in my head. I'm afraid. Deadly afraid.

The examination was lengthy and thorough and conducted, except for medical questions, almost without an exchange of conversation. At the end of it, Wil smiled at me.

'We'll have the results of the blood tests and other specimens in a few days, but I'd venture to say that you're a very healthy young woman. I congratulate you on your sensible attitude about check-ups. So many of us, including me, don't go to the doctor until something hurts.'

'I don't deserve the credit,' I said. 'Roger insisted.'

He raised an eyebrow. 'Oh? Something you haven't told me?'

'Nothing physical.' I hesitated. Then, impulsively, 'Wil, could we talk? Not here. But I need to talk. I *must* talk to someone I trust.'

His face showed genuine concern. 'Nothing wrong between you and Roger, I hope.'

'No. Yes. God, I don't know! But I *have* to know, Wil. Please help me if you can.'

He nodded. 'Of course I will if I can.'

My hands were shaking almost uncontrollably as I

tried to fasten the tiny clasp of the chain, trying to put back my identity. Gently Wil took the little links out of my hand and snapped the hook together. Then he lifted the ring and looked at it.

'It all has something to do with Lila's ring, hasn't it?'

'Then it *is* her ring! I knew you recognized it!'

'Yes. She wore it on a chain, as you do.' He smiled reassuringly. 'Get dressed,' Wil said, 'and we'll go have lunch. Meet you in twenty minutes at Sans Souci, just down the road. I'll tell Roger that things look fine and that I'm taking you out to celebrate, okay?'

'Yes. Thank you, Wil.'

At the door he paused. 'I don't think I can help you much, Virginia. But at least I can listen.'

A few minutes later we were seated in the small, quiet restaurant on the outskirts of town.

'Drink?' Wil asked.

'Not unless you're having one.'

'Wish I could, but I have to go back to work. Let's order, shall we? And then you'd better tell me what's on your mind.'

I told him everything. Some of it he already knew, much of it he did not. He frowned when I told him about the violent retching following tea at Lila's, looked concerned when I related the incident of the frightened horse. But it was not until I confessed that Drew and I had broken into Dolores' studio that he began to look most alarmed.

'I saw all the pictures there, Wil. The pictures of

you and Dolores and Drew. And,' I said blushing, 'I read one of your letters to Dolores. One in which you talked about your child. I didn't mean to pry. I'm so ashamed. And I can understand why you and Dolores could never acknowledge Drew as your son. It must have been hell for you all these years. But it's hell for Drew now. All his anger and resentment is against you and Simon and André. No wonder he's such a strange, mixed-up boy.'

Wil fiddled with his water glass. 'Despite what you saw,' he said finally, 'you mustn't listen to Drew. He's wrong. André is not sterile and Dolores and I are not Drew's parents, Virginia. He was adopted by Dolores and André, but his mother and father are none of us.'

'But the pictures, the letters . . .?'

'Many things can be misinterpreted. Drew adores Dolores. He *wants* her to be his real mother. That's why he has invented this piece of wishful thinking and made it all fit.' He looked at me directly. 'I know. You don't believe me. It's my word against what appears to be pretty concrete evidence to the contrary. But I swear to you, Virginia, that Dolores and I are not the parents of Drew. I loved her. I still love her. Twenty-five years ago I begged her to marry me but she chose André . . . or allowed him to be chosen for her. After she was married, Dolores and I were never lovers again. So you see, we couldn't have conceived Drew.'

'But the pictures . . . the letter,' I said again.

'Dolores and André and I were still very close when they adopted Drew twenty years ago. I guess I still hadn't given up hoping at that point. There were lots of good times for me with Dolores and the baby. We went on picnics, snapped those pictures you saw. Maybe we were subconsciously trying to pretend that we were a family, that Drew was our child. I don't know. We were still terribly in love. But I never touched her after she became Mrs. André Trippe. I couldn't. And then after a while I couldn't stand the hypocritical role of family friend. That's when I stopped going to Madrugada, why I hadn't been there in years until the night I had dinner with you and Roger.'

There was still the letter to be accounted for.

'But your letter to Dolores . . . mentioning your child.'

Wil smiled sadly. 'If you read it again, Virginia, without the influence of Drew, perhaps it wouldn't say exactly what you thought at that emotional moment. I remember writing it. But it doesn't mean what Drew thinks it does.'

I toyed with the salad that had been placed in front of me. Wil correctly read my thoughts.

'It isn't Drew's parentage that troubles you, is it, dear? It's your own. You're trying to put together the meaning of the ring you wear, aren't you? You're wondering why you have Lila's baby ring. By the way, how did you find out it was hers?'

'In the same book with your letter,' I said, 'there was a baby picture of Lila wearing it. And then I figured out that the first letter of each stone spelled

Trippe. What does it mean, Wil? Dolores told me that Lila miscarried a baby that was Josh's, that she had a nervous breakdown because of it. Dolores lied to me, didn't she? Lila had that baby and gave it up for adoption, didn't she? Simon forced her to and Dolores handled the whole thing!' With realization, my voice was rising. '*That's* the child you talked about in the letter, isn't it? Lila's child, not Dolores'. You were trying to help Dolores get through a bad time. She was at school when you wrote that letter! She wasn't even married to André!' I was almost hysterical now. 'It's all true. All the things I feared. I was the baby you mentioned. Lila is my mother and I, God help me, have married her brother!' I was breathing heavily. 'No wonder someone has been trying to kill me. They must know. It's important that I be dead before Roger finds out the truth. That's it, isn't it? Someone has known all along who I am. Someone who discovered this insane coincidence when the damage had already been done!'

Wil reached for my hands and held them tightly. 'Virginia, get hold of yourself!' he ordered. 'None of that is true! Lila did miscarry. You are not her child! Believe me. I swear it!'

'Believe you? How can I believe you or anyone else in this terrible place?' I tried to regain control. For a moment, my voice returned almost to normal. 'All right, Wil. I'll believe you if you'll tell me who the woman was who left me for adoption. Who left me Lila's ring? Who requested that I be named Virginia when Lila's beloved mare was named Virginia Dare – the mare she rode always with Josh Jenkins, the man she loved? I'll believe you, Wil, when you explain how I was born and abandoned in the very place where Lila was a pregnant schoolgirl. Explain those things to me and I'll take your word that Lila Trippe is not my mother.'

He dropped my hands. 'I can't explain it to you, darling,' he said. 'I can only ask you to trust me.'

The words infuriated me. 'Trust you! Why should I trust you or anyone else except my poor, deluded husband? Oh my God, what this will do to Roger! What it will do to *us!*' All my hatred of Simon Trippe came back in a rush of fury. 'Damn Simon Trippe and his precious pride! Damn him for causing his daughter to go out of her mind! Damn him for trying to dispose of me. He's the one. He has to be. Only Simon could frighten Drew into trying to make my horse throw me. Only Simon could make Milesy poison my tea. Only Simon Trippe could take a careful shot at me. He knows everything that's happened to me here! He must have kept track of me all these years and gone crazy when his son married me before he could stop it!'

Wil's voice was urgent. 'No, Virginia! You're all wrong. You're linking a series of unrelated events into a plot against you!'

I laughed harshly. 'That's almost exactly what Señor Trippe said when he came to warn me to mind my own business. He even wanted to know if there was a history of insanity in my family, as though he didn't know that I have a mother who's stark, raving mad!'

Before Wil could say another word I jumped up from the table. 'Well, now I know,' I said. 'And now the great Simon Trippe is going to know that I know.'

I rushed out of the restaurant, Wil running after me, pleading with me to wait. The other diners looked curiously at this spectacle of a hysterical young woman pursued by an imploring, agitated man. At my car I pushed Wil away as he tried to reason with me. I was beyond reason. All I wanted was to come face to face with Simon Trippe, to confront him with my knowledge of his evil. Then I would go away, far away from Madrugada and from the husband I had no right to love.

I started the engine. Wil was still pleading with me. As I drove off, his voice followed me.

'Virginia, wait! There's something more you must know!'

I did not even look back as I headed for the compound for the very last time.

Chapter Twelve

I DROVE recklessly, at breakneck speed, back to Madrugada, sickeningly convinced that everything I had not wanted to believe was true. Even Wil's letter to Dolores made sense in the light of this new discovery. The baby he was talking about was not Drew, not even his and Dolores'. He'd written about 'the' baby, not 'our' baby. He was writing to his beloved to give her courage as she executed Simon's plan to have Lila give her infant up for adoption. It was Dolores who had left me at the adoption center. Dolores who had followed Simon's orders to get rid of his illegitimate grandchild. It must have been some sense of guilt and pity that had made her secretly leave Lila's ring and tell the adoption agency that the baby was to be called Virginia – the name Lila loved.

My mind raced as fast as the car which tore along the road to the compound. All these years Simon had known who adopted his daughter's illegitimate baby. He'd kept track of me. How frustrated and enraged he must have been when, by a weird coincidence, his own son had fallen in love with the Barlow child. I wondered why he had not put a stop to the marriage as soon as he learned of Roger's plans. But how could he, without revealing the 'shameful' behavior of his only daughter? No, in Simon's monstrous mind the solution would be to let me come to this strange place and drive me away. If necessary he would kill me, or have me killed. There'd be no need to explain anything to anyone then. Lila's secret would be kept and the existence of the child known only to himself and Dolores.

Dolores. I winced when I thought of her deceit. I had felt so drawn to her, so sorry for her, forced into a loveless, childless marriage. Now I saw her for what she was – a weakling and a liar. In her 'confession' to me she had falsified the details of Lila's pregnancy. In truth, she had knuckled under to Simon's demands, not only for the adoption arrangements but for the marriage to his son. The act she had put on for me at her house had been very convincing. My lips tightened at the memory of how thoroughly I'd been taken in by it all. And yet, somehow, I couldn't find it in my heart to hate her. Nor could I bring myself to believe that she'd had any part in the conspiracy against me at Madrugada. It was possible that she had no idea that I was Lila's child. The name of the adoptive parents might well have been given to Simon and no one else.

Simon. No wonder he had refused psychiatric help for his daughter. The amnesia brought on by her misery suited her father well. He would make sure that she remembered none of that 'sinful' period. No wonder he'd had Dolores bring her home in her bewildered, foggy state and kept her virtually a prisoner, cutting off all contact with the outside world. Poor Lila. I could not yet think of her as my mother, even though it was bitterly clear that she was the woman who had given birth to me.

With a shock I realized that I had found both of my parents and neither of them knew I was their child. If Lila was my mother, then Josh was my father! Until this moment, I had not even thought that through. Of course he had no idea. If Dolores had told the truth about that part of the story, he did not even know that his beloved Lila had been pregnant.

It added up to a horrifying yet plausible story. Only one piece of it could not be reconciled in my mind. From all accounts – Wil's, Josh's, even Dolores' – Lila had been a strong, almost defiant girl. Why had she agreed to give up her baby? What pressures were so strong that she allowed that to happen?

That part of the puzzle was still missing. Perhaps it was what Wil wanted to tell me as I drove away from the restaurant. I heard his voice calling after me, shouting that there was something more I should know. Everything else added up in my mind except Lila's behavior. But then, how could I possibly imagine what means Simon Trippe had used to get his way? His domination could have, in some unfathomable way, reached out three thousand miles across the country and brought even his headstrong daughter to her knees. Perhaps he had threatened to kill Josh. Nothing less than that would have made Lila part with her baby. Yes. That must have been how it happened. To save the man she loved, Lila had let Dolores put me up for adoption. And having done that she retreated into a world of merciful forgetfulness.

The iron gates of Madrugada came into view now. I sounded the horn impatiently and they opened as they had for André, Roger and me the day I arrived. I drove rapidly to the main house, my only thought to find Simon Trippe and demand a confirmation.

But as I neared the big, gray mansion I saw Simon run out of the front door and jump into a car which sped rapidly off. On the front steps Mrs. Angus was restraining a feeble Natalie Trippe who seemed to be trying to follow her husband. Even at a distance their agitation was obvious. I brought the car to a screeching halt in front of the house and got out, hurrying toward the frightened pair.

'What's wrong, Mrs. Angus? What's happened?'

Wide-eyed, the woman pointed in the direction of the stables. Even at this distance I could see clouds of black smoke and a bright orange sky.

'Fire!' Mrs. Angus said. 'One of the boys came to get Mr. Simon. Everything is going – the barns, the horses. It's even spreading into the woods!'

Natalie Trippe spoke for the first time, her voice

weak and trembling.

'You must let me go,' she said. 'I have to find my baby, my Lila! Please. Take me to her, Virginia.'

Mrs. Angus held the frail woman protectively.

'You can't go out there, Mrs. Trippe,' she said. 'There's nothing you can do. And you're not well enough.'

My anxiety was coupled with confusion. The devastation of a major fire spreading through the stable and into the deep woods was nightmare enough. But what did Lila have to do with this? Why was Natalie pleading that she had to find her daughter?

Mrs. Angus understood my bewilderment. 'We're afraid Miss Lila started it,' she said quietly. 'That's what the boy from the stable said. We don't know how it happened. We only know that she was there and now they can't find her.'

Natalie reached out to me.' 'Please,' she said again, the thin white hands trembling, 'please drive us to the stables. Mr. Trippe wouldn't do it. But I must be there. My child may need me, Virginia. Can't you understand that?'

I wanted to weep for this poor, dying woman.

'Yes, Mrs. Trippe,' I said 'I'll take you. Mrs. Angus, get her something to put around her – a warm coat or a blanket.' Even though the day was hot, the ailing woman was shaking.

Mrs. Angus hesitated. 'I don't think it's wise,' she said. 'Mrs. Trippe is in no condition to leave the house. Besides, Mr. Trippe said . . .'

'To hell with Mr. Trippe!' I exploded. 'Get the coat, Mrs. Angus, while I help Mrs. Trippe into the car!'

The housekeeper went to do my bidding while I gently assisted Natalie to the car. Quickly I put the top up and started the engine. By the time Mrs. Angus returned with a cashmere coat I was ready to drive our odd little trio to the scene of the disaster.

As we came closer to the stable my horror increased. It seemed that the whole world was on fire. Huge flames engulfed the barns and woods and threatened to spread to the nearby buildings. It was a scene of wild confusion as the stablehands led as many of the horses as they could out of their stalls. They had blindfolded the frightened rearing animals, but I knew with a sinking heart that they would never be able to get them all.

Josh, his face blackened and his clothes singed, was shouting directions, while those who were not engaged in trying to save the horses manfully formed a bucket brigade in a futile effort to stop the spread of the inferno. Simon Trippe stood motionless, surveying the holocaust, no sign of emotion on his stern face. Even though I had raced to see him a few minutes earlier, now I couldn't bear to look at him. There was no vestige of humane concern on his stony countenance, certainly no fatherly anxiety about the fate or whereabouts of his only daughter. He glanced briefly at me as I jumped out of the car, his eyes traveling beyond me to see his wife and housekeeper in the front seat of my convertible. But he said nothing. He simply continued to stare at the fire and the frenzied activity as though he were some disinterested and uninvolved passerby.

Frantically I ran to Josh and grabbed his arm. 'Where is she, Josh? Where is Lila?'

He turned an agonized face toward me. 'I don't know. My God, I don't know. She was here and then she disappeared. She may have run into the woods, Virginia.' His voice broke.

I stared at him, horrified. 'But hasn't anyone gone to look for her?'

Tears streamed down Josh's face. 'Mr. Simon has ordered us to stay here and fight the fire until the engine company arrives. He says Lila ran home.' Josh stared at me, dazed. 'He . . . he pointed his gun at me when I told him I was going into the woods to try to find her. He said he'd kill me if I left my job.'

I looked over at Simon. It was true that he held a rifle loosely in his hand. I did not doubt for a moment that he would have used it on Josh or anyone else.

'I'll find her, Josh,' I said.

'No! Virginia, you can't go into those woods! They're going up like a tinder box. The Santa Ana wind is blowing hard. It's spreading the flames faster than anyone can keep up with them.' He was sobbing openly now. 'If Lila is in there she's long since dead. And if you try to go in, that madman will shoot you.'

'He won't shoot me,' I said. 'Not in public.'

I started to run toward the path to the woods,

straight into the trees that were crackling with flames. In three long, rapid strides Simon Trippe suddenly blocked my way.

'I have forbidden anyone to go near those woods,' he said. 'And that includes you.'

For a moment I stopped and stared at him.

'Don't you care that your daughter may be in there?'

'Lila is not in those woods. I told that fool Jenkins that! But even if she were, no one could help her now. I won't see another life needlessly sacrificed, not his or yours.'

I began to laugh hysterically. And then, abruptly, I shoved Simon Trippe with all my might. Caught him off balance, he dropped his rifle.

'You want Lila dead, don't you?' I screamed. 'Just like you want me dead! Well, you won't get your way! I'm going to find my mother!'

I dashed furiously into the woods, too much in shock to be afraid. It was like running into Hell. Burning trees surrounded me and small clumps of flames licked at my feet as I ran, calling Lila. Every few seconds a burning tree limb fell perilously in my path. I dodged around it and pushed heedlessly on into the flaming woods. It was almost impossible to breathe, the intense heat was suffocating me and the wind relentlessly pushed the flames toward me like great, greedy fingers. My clothes clung to my body, glued to me by the furnacelike temperatures. Twice I fell and for a second lay breathless, wondering in those fleeting moments of fear whether I was going to die there. But some fierce determination made me rise and run on deeper into this purgatory. Shouting as I ran, calling Lila's name, I stumbled on, half-blinded by the smoke, not daring to think that it might all be in vain, that perhaps Lila was not even here or that she was already dead. Simon's face seemed to appear before me, saying those very things. He was wrong, I thought. He had to be.

I felt as though I had been on the maniacal journey for hours, though I learned later that it was not more than five minutes that I battled my way through those deadly woods. Then like a mirage I saw a small, cavelike shelter of rocks just ahead of me, only a few feet off the path. It stood like a protective fortress among the crackling greenery. And in it I saw a small still mound – the unconscious figure of Lila.

I raced to this tiny area of refuge and tried to lift the still figure. I could not tell whether she was dead or alive. There was a deep gash in her forehead and the thought crossed my mind that she had stumbled against the protective rocks and fallen unconscious in the one small space that offered a precarious shelter.

With all my strength I tried to lift her, but she was a dead weight and I had barely enough reserve to keep from fainting myself. Praying, I turned and ran back the way I had come. The way was even more perilous, but the path remained passable and my determination so fierce that at last I emerged from the entrance to the woods.

'She's in there!' I yelled. 'In a cave! Somebody help!'

I was aware of Roger and Wil dashing past me and then coming back out, the limp body of Lila between them. They must have arrived seconds after I went into the inferno, I thought irrelevantly. Thank God. And then I blacked out.

When I opened my eyes a few minutes later, Wil was bending over me with such an expression of love and concern that I was startled. Nearby, André tended to Lila as Milesy and Natalie stood by. Behind them, dimly I saw the anguished face of Simon, the grime-streaked remorseful countenance of Josh and a surly, unmoved Drew.

'Roger,' I said weakly. 'Where's Roger?'

My husband was instantly at my side. 'I'm here, darling. Everything is all right now. You're safe.'

I clung to him, feeling the familiar strength of his arms, wondering, even in that dazed moment how I could face the future without him. Remembrance returned, and with it all the despair I felt for the irrevocable, intolerable situation we were now going to have to face. Ironic that the mother I had searched for all my life had proven to be the vehicle of my greatest unhappiness. I looked up at Roger.

'Lila,' I said. 'Is she all right?'

'Yes, thanks to you.' Roger glanced toward the little circle surrounding the unconscious woman. 'The head wound looks superficial. I'm sure she'll be fine.'

I sat up. My own head was clearing now and I felt no

more than a slight shakiness from the dangerous rescue of a few minutes before. The fire on the property was under control but portions of the woods continued to blaze. Men from the village were fighting to contain it, hampered by the great gusts of winds that came sweeping across the hills. I could see them digging trenches to stop the merciless spread of the flames. The big stable was virtually gutted but the nearby buildings where the staff lived seemed only slightly damaged.

'They got all but two of the horses out,' Roger assured me, 'but the tack room where the fire started is completely destroyed. Poor Josh. Thirty years of ribbons and trophies gone in seconds. It's like wiping out most of his life. Thank God nobody was hurt. That's all that matters.'

'What happened?' I asked. 'Did Lila really start it?'

'We don't know. Somehow she slipped away from Milesy this afternoon and came out here. The first time she's done such a thing since she was a girl. Josh knew she shouldn't be wandering around alone, so he left her in the tack room for a moment to go next door and call Milsey. When he came back the room was on fire and Lila was running away. The Señor was sure she was making her way back home but instead, as you know, she wandered into the woods. Thank God you went after her, darling.'

I did not tell him what Josh had said nor how Simon had threatened anyone who wanted to go looking for Lila.

'But why would Lila set fire to the stables?' I asked. 'She loved them so, just as . . .' I stopped. I had almost said, 'just as she loved Josh.'

'It must have been an accident,' Roger answered. 'Like a child playing with matches. When the fire started she got frightened and ran. Lila can't be held responsible for her actions. You know that.'

I stood up. 'I want to see her,' I said.

With Roger's arm around me, I walked slowly to the spot where Lila lay. As we came near, she opened her eyes and looked at the concerned faces above her, her gaze finally coming to rest on Josh's tender, grateful face. The voice was almost a whisper, but it was distinct and womanly, a far cry from the little-girl tone in which Lila usually spoke.

'Michael,' she said softly, looking into Josh's eyes, 'we lost our baby.'

Before he could answer, Milesy reached out her arms to Lila.

'It's all right, sweetheart,' she said. 'You're safe with Milesy now.'

Lila ignored her as completely as though she were a total stranger. Instead, the woman on the ground held a weak hand out to Natalie Trippe.

'Mother, I fell,' she said. 'The jump was too high. My baby was born dead. My poor little baby.'

Natalie knelt and took her into her arms, cradling her like a child, her tears falling on Lila's pathetic face.

'I know, darling. I know. You couldn't help it. Try

to rest, Lila dear. Mother will stay with you.' Natalie seemed to call on some deep reserve of strength. She did not even appear stunned by the strange words. 'Roger, André, take your sister home,' she said. 'To *my* house.' With the last words Natalie looked defiantly at Simon. 'That's where Lila belongs,' she said 'That's where she's always belonged.'

Obediently, her sons lifted the injured woman gently and carried her to André's car. Natalie was in command now. 'Go with them, Josh,' she said. 'Lila needs you.' Then Mrs. Trippe turned to me. 'You're in no condition to drive, child. Mrs. Angus will take me back in your car. Drew will see you home in his. Simon, are you coming?'

Her husband did not look at her. 'No,' he said,' 'not now. I'll stay to supervise the men.'

'As you like,' Natalie said. I had never seen such dignity and control. Was this the helpless, frightened, sick woman I'd known? Sick, yes. Nothing could change that. But fierce maternal protectiveness had overcome the timidity and diffidence she'd projected since the day we met. Lila's sudden recognition of her seemed to give the confidence that I'd not known was within her. In this moment she, not Simon, was the head of the Trippe family. I looked at her, strong, calm, decisive. A voice of sanity in the midst of panic. She was like an older Dolores, capable and assured. And in that strange moment I realized that she knew about the love between Lila and Josh. That she'd always known and until now had not dared to admit it.

I knew something else, too. Something that hit me like a beautiful, wonderful reprieve. I was not Lila's child. The full impact of her words came back to me. 'My baby was born dead,' she'd told her mother. Intuitively, I knew she spoke the truth. For that moment, at least, she was lucid. Every ounce of my being told me so. Every bit of the nurses' training I'd received told me that these words came from the innermost reaches of a mind slowly trying to reach out once again for reality. My relief was overwhelming. It was like awakening from a bad dream. 'Michael, we lost our baby,' she'd said. 'Lost it' in the way that death, not adoption, is a loss. It was said with such sadness, such finality that the meaning was clear. I had been around too many women in the hospital not to know that when they miscarried the expression they inevitably used was: 'I lost the baby.'

Tears were close to my eyes. Tears of sadness for this tortured woman and, selfishly, tears of joy for myself. An intense surge of gratitude filled my breast. I was free. Free of my terrible conviction. Free to be a wife to the man I loved. I thought only fleetingly of the ring and my name. I did not know how I had come by them. Somehow I was tied into Lila's life, but not in the way I'd feared. I felt only curiosity now; not the agonizing belief I had endured all these weeks. I would go to Dolores and demand a full explanation. I looked around, surprised to realize that Dolores had not been at the scene of the near-tragedy. It struck me as odd. Everyone else had come racing to the stables when they heard that Lila was missing. Even Drew. It was impossible that Dolores did not know what was happening. And unthinkable that she would ignore it.

A hand on my elbow interrupted these musings.

'My *orders* are to see you home,' Drew said sarcastically. 'Ready to go?'

I nodded, suddenly numb with fatigue. Wearily, I climbed into Drew's car, longing to get home and sleep for hours. Time later to talk to Roger and Dolores. Time to see whether, as I hoped, the blow to Lila's head might be the beginning of recovery. I had read of cases where amnesia continued for years, only to be cured by a similar recurrence of the thing that caused it.

I leaned back against the seat and shut my eyes. The soft air brushed against my face and the setting sun glimmered gently against my closed lids. I was glad that Drew kept the top down on his convertible. It was good to feel the fresh, clean, cool breeze of oncoming evening. It lulled me as he drove slowly away from the stables. Neither of us spoke. And before I knew it, I had dropped off to sleep, exhausted from all that happened that fateful afternoon.

Chapter Thirteen

IT WAS dark when I awoke, startled to find that we were still driving. I did not recognize the winding road we were on, a road that headed high up into the mountains away from Madrugada. I had no idea how long I'd been asleep. Long enough, I was sure, to take me many miles from home.

For a few seconds I was too astonished to be frightened. The headlights picked out the narrow dirt road we were on. Everything was eerily quiet, dark and deserted. Only the steady hum of the car engine broke the stillness. Sensing my movements, Drew momentarily took his eyes from the road to glance at me. It was an unfathomable look, full of determination and hatred and yet somehow reflecting reluctance and fear as well.

'So you finally woke up.'

'Drew! For God's sake, where are we?'

He concentrated on his driving. 'What difference does it make?'

'What difference! You were supposed to drive me

home. What are we doing up here in these God-forsaken hills?'

He held the wheel with one hand, wiping the other on the side of his trousers. I saw that he was sweating profusely though the night air was so chilly that I shivered with cold. Or perhaps, I realized, I had begun to shake with fright. With sickening certainty I knew the answer to my own question: Drew Trippe had brought me up into the mountains to kill me.

I turned in the seat and looked behind me, hoping desperately for some sign of light. Perhaps I could jump out of the car and run to safety in the woods. Drew was driving very slowly, very carefully. But the world around us was plunged into total blackness. Even if I tried to escape, Drew would catch me in a minute. My only hope was to attempt to reason with my insane kidnapper, and a very faint hope it was.

'Drew,' I said quietly, 'what is this all about?'

'I imagine you must have guessed by now.' He laughed mirthlessly. 'After all, we've struck out three times. We didn't frighten you off. So now we have to get rid of you once and for all.'

'We?' I echoed. 'Who is "we"?'

'We is my mother and me.'

'Your mother! I don't believe it! Not Dolores!'

He drove for a few minutes and then pulled the car off the side of the road. As though we were making small talk at a cocktail party, he put his arm across the back of the seat and half-turned, facing me conversationally.

'Dolores isn't my mother,' he said. 'All that garbage I fed you in the studio was a pack of lies. That letter you read from Wiseman to Dolores wasn't about me. It was about you.'

I stared at him, uncomprehending.

'Dolores and Wiseman are *your* parents, Virginia,' he said. 'Not mine.'

'But I don't understand,' I stammered. 'How could that be? And how could you know it, even if it were true?'

'It's true, all right. Like Dolores told you, Lila was pregnant by Josh when she went off to school in the East. But what Dolores didn't tell you was that she was pregnant too. By Wil Wiseman. Dolores knew she had to have an abortion because she had to marry André. Save the old family homestead, that kind of thing. But when Lila took her spill, miscarried and lost her memory, Dolores saw a way to save her own baby, even if she couldn't ever acknowledge it. She had the child – you – and placed it for adoption as Lila's baby. Even left the ring, which she took from Lila, and gave you Lila's favorite name. Lila knew nothing. She'd fallen, miscarried and blacked out. It was easy for Dolores to keep her hospitalized long enough for you to be born. Then Dolores told Simon that Lila had had a baby and the two of them arranged for it to be left for adoption. That's when Wil Wiseman wrote the letter you read. The letter was about Dolores' decision to have you. He wanted his child kept alive even if he could never see it or ever marry Dolores.'

I tried to absorb this complicated story. There was no way that I could be sure that Drew was telling the truth even now. Yet it did fit. It would have been easy for Dolores, far away and alone with a girl who remembered nothing, to do just what Drew had suggested. Dolores and Wil knew the name of the people who adopted 'Lila's' baby. They could have kept track of me all these years, wanting to know the fate of their child. That was what Wil had decided to tell me as I drove furiously away from the restaurant this afternoon.

Drew seemed more relaxed now, almost enjoying my bewilderment as I tried to absorb what he had told me. Finally, I turned to him imploringly.

'But I still don't understand. You said "we". Who is it that wants me dead? And why?'

'I told you. My mother and I want you dead. *My* mother is *your* mother's only friend – Carmelita. Dolores told her the whole story when she and Andrew adopted me. Dolores couldn't have other children. I'm the product of the housekeeper and a Mexican stable boy, but to the world I'm the sole heir to the Trippe fortune. Carmelita wanted that for her child. That's why she gave me up. She wasn't going to stand quietly by and see Roger produce real grandchildren for Simon. When you came, it was Carmelita's idea to scare you off and then eventually kill Roger. But we failed three times: once when Carmelita visited Milesy and put just enough poison in your tea; and the last time when you were lucky enough to stay on that damned horse instead of getting thrown as I planned. Incidentally, I made sure Simon heard about the "accidents" so he'd be sure your interpretation of them was neurotic.

'When those things didn't work, we decided to drive you away by making you think you'd married your mother's brother. It was easy. Rosita told Carmelita about your ring. My mother saw it and recognized it. All I had to do was to show you the picture in the album and let you take it from there.' Drew laughed. 'It damned near worked, too. If Lila hadn't babbled that stuff about her dead baby, you'd have divorced Roger and gone away. It would have been easy to get rid of him after that. A fake suicide, despair over your leaving. Now we have a double job to do. Two murders are too hard to explain, so it'll have to be two suicides. First, they'll find you hanging from a tree. Later they'll find Roger dead, unable to live without you. Simon is conditioned to think you're half-crazy. He'll buy your suicide and his son's, too. Particularly with Lila's history.'

It was dark now. Drew had turned the car lights off and only a sliver of a moon outlined the demented face as he outlined the twisted plan that he and Carmelita had devised to insure his inheritance.

'You'll never get away with it,' I said. 'Dolores and Wil are bound to tie the whole thing back to Carmelita, the only other person who knows about me. Even if they've never acknowledged me, Drew, they'll not see their child's murderer go free.'

'They'll also believe you committed suicide,' Drew said easily. 'You've seen to that. I'm sure you've already told Wil that you think Lila is your mother.'

It was a wild guess but my face betrayed the accuracy of it. Drew was right. After the scene I'd made today, Wil would believe that I'd destroyed myself in despair over my incestuous marriage. And Roger's guilty taking of his own life later would be sadly accepted. It would go just the way Carmelita planned it, with nothing but agony for Dolores and Wil, death for Roger and me.

I began to plead, not only for my life but for Roger's. I swore to Drew that I would go away and make Roger go with me, that we would assign our share of the estate to Drew, that we would forfeit any right to inheritance. I can do it, I promised. I can make Roger relinquish any claim, even if we have children of our own. He'll agree to the bargain, I insisted, when he knows that our lives depend upon it. I knew it was futile, but I had to try.

Drew only laughed.

'What kind of a fool do you think I am?' he said. 'Sorry, Virginia. I really almost liked you. Who knows? I might even have given up the idea of the total inheritance and been satisfied with what Dolores and André leave me. But I can't do that to my mother. This is what she wants. She's sacrificed everything for me. The least I can do is to become the Patron of Madrugada, even if she doesn't live to see it. I mean, I know I have to survive Simon and Natalie as well as Dolores and André. But that shouldn't be a problem. Simon's an old man and Natalie is dying. As for my adoptive parents, well, if they last too long there's a way around that, too.'

He's completely mad, I thought. I am at the mercy of a lunatic. Still, I stalled for time.

'Drew, you can't mean what you're saying. You're no murderer. You're certainly not a mass murderer! You'd even have to get rid of Lila if her competency is restored! You'd never get away with such a plan. Somewhere along the way you'd trip yourself up. Do what you said,' I begged. 'Settle for your inheritance from Dolores and André. I give you my word that Roger and I will still go away. And I swear to you on my solemn oath that I'll never tell what was said here tonight.'

He shook his head. 'No deal.' He glanced at the radium dial of his watch. It was past eight o'clock. We'd been gone for more than two hours. By now they must be searching for us, I thought. If only I can keep delaying, maybe Roger or Wil or someone will find us. The thought led me to one more appeal to Drew.

'We'll have been missed by now,' I said. 'They'll know, when they find me, that you did it.'

'I don't think so. You see, it may be days before they find you. I'll say that I dropped you off at your house. Rosita will swear to that. Carmelita will see that she does. Then I'll say that after I took you home

I drove into town the way I've done every night for weeks.' He smiled. 'It was nice of you to provide me with an alibi, by the way. Didn't you suggest to Dolores that my long, unexplained absences probably had to do with some girl in the city? I can explain these hours easily. Of course, they'll wonder how you left your house and got up here in the mountains to commit suicide by hanging yourself from that tree over there, but they'll never figure it out.'

He reached in the back seat and took out a long rope and a red bandana. Roughly he grabbed my arms and, with the scarf, bound my wrists tightly behind my back.

'Nice touch, huh?' Drew said. 'Too bad I can't leave it behind. Get out of the car,' he said, leaning across me to open the door on my side.

'Drew! No! I beg you!'

He shoved me out of the car. 'Shut up! There's been too much talking already.'

Hypnotized, I watched him make a hangman's noose on the branch of a nearby tree. I was going to die a horrible death and I was powerless to stop it. With terrible fascination I saw him approach me. Almost as an afterthought, he pulled the chain with Lila's ring off my throat, roughly removed my engagement and wedding rings and put them in his pocket.

'Just had a good idea,' he said. 'Might as well add another red herring. If the police don't buy the suicide theory they'll go for robbery and murder. They'll figure you were dazed by the fire, wandered out on the road and got picked up by some stranger who took your jewelry and then drove you up here and killed you. That's terrific,' he said proudly. 'I told Carmelita that we couldn't count on the suicide theory. Need to throw as much doubt on your death as we can. She'll be proud of me.'

My throat had gone dry with terror. When my voice came out it was almost a whispered croak.

'Don't do it this way, please,' I said. 'If you're determined to kill me, then for God's sake be merciful, Drew. Put a bullet in my head and have done with it.'

'Bullets can be traced. Too risky. Besides, that would eliminate suicide. There'd have to be a gun beside you.'

It was true, I realized dully, that one's life did pass before one's eyes at the moment of death. I saw clearly my early, happy life with the Barlows, my romance and marriage to Roger, the active days at the hospital back East when even the hardest physical work was not too much for a healthy, strong girl such as I.

And then I saw it, the first glimmer of hope. Far down the road I was sure that I saw the headlights of a car. They were tiny pin points approaching us. Someone was searching for me but they would never get to me in time.

I waited, watching intently for my chance. When all was in readiness, Drew came close to me.

'It's time,' he said.

With a sudden rapid movement I lunged at him, butting him in the stomach with my head. The force of the blow knocked him backward for an instant, just as a few hours earlier I had shoved Simon out of the way when he tried to stop me from going to look for Lila. I took advantage of the split second of surprise and began to run down the road, hands tied behind me, screaming, stumbling, half-falling on the dark, treacherous path. I yelled at the top of my voice, my cries filling the dark, empty night. Drew was in immediate pursuit. Within a hundred yards he'd caught me and thrown me angrily to the ground. He leaned over me, breathing heavily. Then he pulled me roughly to my feet.

'Get back up there,' he ordered.

Helplessly I made my way back to the tree, praying for time. Twice I deliberately fell, only to be yanked upright and pushed on. But each time I dropped to the ground I looked backward. The headlights were getting closer. Drew, absorbed in his terrible task, had not seen them. It was not until we were back at the base of the big tree and he was preparing to drop the noose over my head that he heard the car. It was coming fast now. Somone began leaning on the horn. The lights had picked us out and above the strident blare I could hear a man's voice shouting.

Drew seemed paralyzed by the oncoming vehicle. He stood frozen, the rope in one hand while the other held my arm in a bone-crushing grip. And then Wil

Wiseman was upon us.

The next few moments were a blur to me. I remember only Wil jumping out of the car and smashing his fist into Drew's face. I felt Wil untying my hands and gathering me protectively into his arms, saying over and over, 'My god, baby. My God, my God! What have we done to you?' I was dimly aware that a woman had jumped out of the car seconds later, a woman who ran to me and put her arms around us both. In my last moments of consciousness I realized that it was Dolores, tears streaming down her face.

When I came to I was in my own bed. Wonderingly I touched the soft covers as though to reassure myself that I was safe. Roger, Wil and Dolores stood nearby, looking anxiously down at me.

'Welcome back, sweetheart,' my husband said.

I tried to answer, but the words came out in disconnected, confused gasps.

'Where . . . how . . . Drew . . .'

'Hush,' Roger said. 'Time for all that when you've had a good rest. I'm going to give you a sedative, darling. I don't want any talking now. Time enough for that tomorrow.'

I felt a needle go into my arm and then blessed oblivion. Even in those last fuzzy seconds, a wonderful thought struck me. I'm with my real family at last. I smiled and slipped off into a dreamless sleep.

When I awakened it was a peaceful morning. Sunshine flooded my room. I was alone. Only the rumpled place beside me told me that Roger had been close to me all through the night. I lay still, trying to reconstruct, not the horror of those hours in the hills with Drew, but the revelations he had thought he was confiding to a woman who would not live to repeat them. I prayed that the ravings of my young abductor were true. I would not be completely convinced until I heard the story confirmed by the two he said were my parents.

Unthinkingly, I rang the little bedside bell which summoned Rosita. Instead it was Roger who came quietly into the room, took me into his arms and held me to him. Then he released me and tried to smile.

'Rosita won't be answering any more darling,' he said. 'She's already been sent packing . . . along with Carmelita.'

It began to come back slowly. Of course. Rosita had always been part of the plan . . . a plan that started even before I came to Madrugada. It was her aunt who had so 'thoughtfully' provided me with a housekeeper who was a spy. I remembered the eavesdropping, now. The frightened, near-slips of the tongue whenever she mentioned Carmelita. Strangely, I felt sorry for the girl. She was obviously terrified of her aunt, probably an unwilling accomplice to Carmelita's deranged scheme.

It was hard to believe that the kind, efficient Carmelita was the mastermind behind the plot against me. But it was so. It was Carmelita blindly fighting for her son's inheritance, Carmelita encouraging Drew, instructing him in how to get rid of me. The confidante of a trusting Dolores and the Svengali of a terrified Rosita, only Carmelita could have kept such a close watch on me. The 'faithful servant,' she had access to all the houses. Milesy probably thought nothing of it when she went into the kitchen that day to prepare tea and found that Carmelita had already set up the cups that Lila and Milesy regularly used and had even poured the extra one for their visitor. I now understood the reason for Simon Trippe's unexpected visit to my house in his wife's place. Rosita had told Carmelita and Carmelita had informed Simon who was determined to protect his dying wife from emotional distress.

I had understandably misjudged Simon. Harsh and misguided as he was, he held no enmity toward me. I was certain that Dolores had not told the truth. Simon knew that Lila miscarried. He'd had no fears that I was his grandchild. He was merely a disappointed man, frustrated that Roger had not married someone of a good California family.

'I owe your father an apology,' I said to Roger. 'I was wrong about him. He never hated me. I see that now. But he did deliberately withhold treatment from Lila.' My voice saddened. 'And Dolores allowed it. It was her protection against the only person who might have spoken the truth about that abandoned baby.' My eyes filled with tears. 'How could she, Roger? How could she be so cruel to Lila and to me? My own mother. And I admired her so.'

He put his hand gently over my mouth. 'Don't you think you should withhold judgment until you hear her side? She and Wil and I talked for hours last night after you went to sleep. It's an amazing story, Virginia, and a sad one. But give her a chance to tell you about it herself.'

I turned away from him. 'Nothing she could say would justify what she did.'

'Perhaps not,' Roger said. 'But she deserves a hearing. You do want to hear the whole story from her, don't you?'

I didn't answer. I did want to hear the story from her and from my father as well. But I dreaded facing the final reality of her abandonment of me, her selfish use of Lila, the heartache she'd caused Wil all these years.

'Yes,' I said finally, 'I want to hear it all.'

'Good girl. Now how about some good news? That fall in the woods seems to have reversed Lila's amnesia. She's remembering bits and pieces now. She knows Josh – Michael as she calls him – and slowly she's recalling what happened. These last twenty-five years are a blank to her, of course, but she's rediscovered her love, Virginia. We'll get help for her. It might be a long road, but she'll make it.'

'I'm glad. Josh still loves her so much. And Simon won't interfere?'

Roger shook his head. 'He's overcome with gratitude that Lila has come back to us. Whatever he felt about Josh's unsuitability is no longer important to him.'

'What about Drew?' The mere mention of his name made me go cold with remembered fear.

'He's to be institutionalized, dear. He's a very sick young man. As for Carmelita, perhaps we're too softhearted, but if you agree, we've decided to simply let her go back to Mexico. She did what she thought she had to do to protect her son's inheritance. There was no hope for him otherwise. A terrible thing. But then mothers sometimes will go to any lengths for the welfare of their children, dangerous and wrong as their actions may be. Carmelita is a broken woman. She'll live with the terrible knowledge of what she tried to do. That's punishment enough, I think. She's not a murderess, Virginia. She was desperate, but she'll never have reason again to harm another person. And she was like part of our family for more than twenty years.' He looked at me carefully. 'It's up to you, my love. You were the one who nearly died because of her. If you want us to, we'll prosecute. She can be sent to jail for conspiracy and attempted murder. Drew can be tried, too, though he'll be committed in any case. The decision is yours. We'll do what you want.'

For a moment I was torn by a very human desire for revenge, but Roger's gentle face made me ashamed.

'No,' I said. 'Let her go. God help her.'

He kissed me gently. 'I love you, Virginia Trippe.'

Chapter Fourteen

ROGER GAVE orders that I was not to be disturbed for twenty-four hours. One of the nurses from the clinic was brought over to see to my needs while I stayed in bed. I was anxious to see Dolores and Wil, to witness Lila's first steps toward recovery, and to tell Natalie how much I admired her. But my husband was firm.

'No talking for one full day,' he said. 'Doctor's orders. You've had a terrible, traumatic experience. I want you to get your strength and your perspective before you talk to anybody but me.'

I protested. 'I'm fine. Roger, you *must* understand how important it is for me to talk to Dolores and Wil, at least.'

'Tomorrow,' he said. 'You've waited twenty-five years to talk to your parents. You can survive another day.'

'You're not telling me the truth,' I said suddenly. 'It's they who don't want to talk to me.'

'They're terrified by the prospect,' Roger said calmly, 'but it's the most important thing in their lives . . . talking to you. They love you, Virginia. They hope to make you understand and, most of all if you can, to forgive them.' He paused. 'They have a few things to make right in their own lives, too.'

I had to be content with that for another day. Actually, I knew that Roger was right. I was still too emotionally and physically exhausted from my brush with death to face anyone. Sedated, I slept most of the time, waking only to take a little nourishment and drifting off again into restorative forgetfulness.

On the second morning I felt well and strong, and yet when Roger came to tell me that Dolores and Wil were waiting, I became almost physically ill with nervousness.

They were seated together on the living room sofa, holding hands, looking surprisingly young and anxious. I was struck again by what an extraordinarily attractive pair they were, Dolores with her patrician beauty, her blondness a dramatic contrast to Wil's dark, passionate good looks. Both wore casual clothes, silk shirts open at the the throat and slim, well-tailored slacks. They seemed frightened and vulnerable and hardly old enough to be my parents.

We greeted each other awkwardly, almost formally. A far different reunion than the emotional one we'd had on that lonely, terror-filled mountain road.

'Thank you for saving me from Drew,' I said stiffly. 'How did you know where we were?'

'Thank your . . . thank Dolores,' Wil said. 'When

Roger found that you weren't at home, he called her to see whether she knew where Drew had gone. Rosita had sworn that he dropped you off there.'

'I knew, instinctively, that something was wrong,' Dolores said, picking up the story, 'so I questioned Carmelita. I . . . I threatened to kill her if she didn't tell me the whole truth. She knew I meant it. I think I would have killed her. That's when she told me that Drew knew everything, that she'd told him about Wil and me, about you and about his own parentage. She was like a wild woman.' Dolores shuddered. 'She poured out the whole thing. How they planned to frighten you away. And when that failed, how they planned to kill you.'

'I think her mind finally snapped after these tense months,' Wil said. 'I suppose that's why she spilled the whole plan. Or maybe she really did fear for her life. Anyway, Dolores called me immediately and we came looking for you.' He rubbed his hand across his eyes. 'The timing was nothing short of a miracle. My God, when I think what would have happened if Dolores hadn't been intuitive about Carmelita's part in this . . . or if we'd been five minutes later!'

'You weren't at the fire,' I said irrelevantly. 'Where were you, Dolores?'

'In Los Angeles. I got home just after you saved Lila. Carmelita was there, but she kept out of sight. It was when Natalie ordered Drew to drive you home that she and her son decided on the last desperate move.' Dolores buried her face in her hands. 'What a fool I was to confide in her all these years! But I had to talk to someone. Beside Wil, I mean. I was so consumed with guilt, Virginia. I'd told so many lies, covered up so much. I'm not a formally religious person but I needed a confessor, even though no one could forgive me for my sins.

'When Carmelita became pregnant I begged her to let André and me adopt that child because I knew I couldn't have any more. I promised her that Drew would have the security she could never give him, and that she could always be near him in our house. She agreed, for her son's future. Her motives for parting with her child were a great deal more noble than mine.'

Wil was instantly protective. 'Your reasons were different but no less noble, darling,' he said. 'You see, Virginia, Dolores' father had stolen money from Simon's firm. If she had refused to marry André, Simon would have disgraced Mr. Del Cruz. Maybe even had him imprisoned. Dolores couldn't let that happen, even though it meant sacrificing herself and you . . . and me. If anyone was ignoble in all this, it was I. I should have gone to Simon and told him the truth about Dolores and me and our baby. I should have offered to repay the money, somehow, some way. But I was a poor, struggling doctor in those days. It was hopeless to think that I could ever replace the hundreds of thousands of dollars Mr. Del Cruz had taken. Dolores wouldn't let me even approach Simon. She was terrified of him. As everyone is. Or was.'

'By the time my father died, it was too late to do anything,' Dolores went on. 'You were a grown girl, already enrolled in nursing school. Wil and I had always kept track of you. We knew what wonderful people the Barlows are, how happy you were. We convinced ourselves that we had no right to disrupt your life after all these years.'

Disrupt my life. If only they knew how I had ached to find out who I was. An awkward silence fell over the room. I tried to sort out my own feelings toward these newly discovered parents. I could see how their problems had seemed insurmountable, how they had tried to do the 'right thing' even at the sacrifice of their own happiness, but I could not understand how they could have abandoned me, no matter how confused and frightened they were.

As though she read my thoughts, Dolores said sadly, 'Leaving my child, my love child, was the greatest sin of my life. And I've paid for it a thousand times over. I'm still paying for it. And so are so many others, Virginia dear. It's why Wil has never married. Why I've unfairly only gone through the motions of being a wife to André. Why André has become a hard bitter man. He didn't know it, but in my own mind I've never been "married" to anyone but Wil.' Her eyes brimmed with tears. 'I know now that I did a wrong, unfair thing, penalizing so many people to save my father. I had no excuse except that I was terribly young and intimidated. I didn't dare think of the future. I was only looking for a way to salvage the present.'

My mind throbbed with questions. 'What about Lila? Did Simon know she miscarried? Or did you lie to me about all that?'

Dolores took the stinging accusation without flinching. 'Yes, I lied to you. I didn't dream you'd reach the conclusions you did. Simon knew nothing of Lila's pregnancy. No one did. I'm sure that Natalie suspected the romance between Lila and Josh, but Simon did not even know that much. He accepted the fall, the resultant brain damage. There was never any talk of pregnancy or miscarriage, much less of adoption.'

'But you let Simon believe that Lila couldn't be helped! How could you do such a thing? Was it because that was the only way your own secret was safe?'

Dolores was aghast. 'No! I swear to you that every doctor told me she had no chance of recovery. You must believe that! I took advantage of it, I admit, to keep her hospitalized in the East long enough for me to have you and place you for adoption as her child. But I told Simon that she was incurable because I believed it. Every specialist confirmed it. As God is my judge, Virginia, I wouldn't have let Lila pay such a price! I lied to you the day we had lunch because keeping my secret has become second nature to me. I never dreamed that Drew would show you the photograph of Lila and the baby ring. I had no idea he'd ever been in the studio.'

'Why did you leave the ring?' I asked. 'And why did you specify that I was to be named Virginia?'

'I'm not sure,' Dolores said. 'I suppose I thought that if somehow my secret ever was discovered those two things would fortify my story that you were Lila's child. It was her ring. And, of course, everyone knew about Virginia Dare.' She laughed mirthlessly. 'The false clues worked all too well. When you found them you jumped to the conclusion that must have nearly driven you out of your mind. But, of course, I never dreamed that it would be you who would try to put the pieces together. I thought no one ever would. Least of all you.'

A strange suspicion crossed my mind. 'You kept track of me. Did you arrange for me to meet Roger?' Wil answered. 'No. Roger knew nothing. That was one of those strange quirks of fate. Of course, when we heard about it we were overjoyed. It was like a miracle. Like Divine forgiveness. After all these years, the chance to be near our own child seemed a sign of God's mercy, a blessing we never dared hope to receive. We talked of how wonderful it would be just to see you, knowing that you were ours, even if no one else knew.'

'No one,' Dolores said, 'except Carmelita. I trusted her so completely. I had to share the happy news with her. I should have foreseen her reaction. You were a threat to Drew. You would produce babies who would be legitimate, not adopted Trippe heirs. That's when she decided that no one would stand in her child's way. And you and Roger almost died because of it.'

Roger intervened. 'You can't blame youself for that, Dolores. Don't you see it wouldn't have mattered whom I'd married? The outcome would have been the same, no matter whom I'd brought as a bride to Madrugada. Carmelita's threat was *any* child of mine. She'd have done the same even if my wife had not been Virginia. I was the one who had to be killed before I could father an heir. The attempts on Virginia's life were just a roundabout way to get at the important victim – me.'

They were looking at me now. And suddenly all the anger I'd felt toward the mother who'd deserted me, all the resentment toward the father who did not interfere, all the self-pity and sense of rejection seemed to leave me. They'd been foolish, even cowardly people, but I could not hate them. I saw Dolores not as my mother but as a frightened young girl torn between love and filial loyalty. I saw Wil helpless in the face of a seemingly unsolvable dilemma. I even felt a twinge of pity for André, ignorant of the reasons for Dolores' inability to love him, disappointed by her barrenness, embittered by the happiness he could read so clearly on the face of his younger brother. I felt saddened by all this misguided misery, but as I looked at my parents I recognized the stirring of a deep affection that I knew would grow into love. It would take time to accept them without reservation, to fully forgive them for the deprivation I'd lived with all my life. But it would happen. With a great rush of happiness I realized that all the years of wondering and searching were over, all the dreadful fears about my origins behind me. I was free. And in giving me my freedom they had regained their own.

I went to them and knelt on the floor in front of the sofa, taking their hands in mine.

'I've looked for you for such a long time. I'm so grateful we've finally found each other.'

Weeping openly, Dolores put her arms around me, then released me for Wil's embrace. I could feel his heart beating with happiness. Or was it, I wondered, my own?

It was Roger who injected a practical note into this emotional scene.

'What happens now? With you two, I mean.'

Dolores looked at Wil, waiting for him to answer.

'We're going to see André. Tell him the whole story. Dolores will get a divorce and we'll have the rest of our lives together. I hope André will find a new life, too. He's still a young man. He deserves happiness, a wife who cares for him and children of his own.'

Roger nodded. 'It's the greatest kindness you can do him. I'm sure he'll want to stay on here. He's the only one of us, except Simon, who really loves this place. He's the right one to inherit Madrugada and leave it to his own flesh and blood.'

I looked inquiringly at my husband.

'Yes, darling,' Roger said, 'we're going away, too.

We don't belong here. You've known that from the first. I was the selfish one who didn't want to admit how stifling and inbred this life has to be for a girl like you.'

'And Lila and Josh?' I asked.

'That will take longer,' Roger said, 'but with psychiatric treatment we think Lila will completely recover. I spoke to Josh yesterday. He's a patient and loving man. When Lila is well enough, he'd like to take her to Kentucky. He had an open job offer there any time he wants it. He's always wanted to go, but, like Wil, he stayed to be near the only woman he could ever love.'

'Even though she didn't even know him,' I said sadly.

'He knew her,' Roger answered quietly. 'I think he never lost faith.'

I nodded, remembering the conversation with Josh my first day at the stables. I heard once again his bemused review of Lila's accident, the questioning and disbelief that I now recognized as a refusal to accept the verdict of hopelessness.

That very night, Roger and I packed our clothes in preparation for the honeymoon we'd never had. We would go for a month to Hawaii then settle in Los Angeles where Wil and Roger would go into practice together. I would work as their nurse until I began to have babies.

We made two calls before we left the compound.

The first stop was Lila's little house to which its owner had returned. She was propped up in bed, holding tightly to the hand of a happy Josh who sat beside her. Though she seemed vague and disoriented, the 'little girl' was gone. In place of the teen-ager was a calm, quiet woman who nodded contentedly as the man she loved explained who we were.

'You saved my life,' Lila said. 'Thank you.'

There was a lump in my throat as I kissed her. 'I helped,' I said. 'But more importantly, you saved mine.'

The big eyes looked uncomprehending.

'Never mind, darling,' Josh said. 'I'll explain it to you later. We'll take it slowly, right, sweetheart?' He turned to Roger and me. 'She's going to get the best therapy there is. We start with a fine psychiatrist as soon as she's able. Mr. Trippe wants nothing but happiness for her.' Josh grinned impishly. 'Hell, he even wants me.'

Feeling as though we'd witnessed a rebirth, Roger and I drove to our last stop – the main house. Hand-in-hand we walked to the front door. As she had on that first visit, Mrs. Angus opened it. But now she was not the overpowering, forbidding figure I had seen. There was a gentle smile on her face as she beckoned us in.

'I was so hoping you'd come,' she said. 'They've been waiting anxiously all evening. Mr. André was here earlier and told them everything.'

'How is Mrs. Trippe?' I asked.

'She's an amazing lady, Miss Virginia. She knows she's dying but she's serene and stronger about it than Mr. Trippe.'

The housekeeper led the way into the little room adjoining the gloomy salon. Natalie sat quietly working on her needlepoint. Simon stood staring out the window into the star-filled night. I had not seen either of them since the fire and it seemed to me that in those forty-eight hours a change had come over these two elderly people. Natalie appeared to have retained the confidence and purpose she'd shown on that terrible afternoon and added to it a new peacefulness with no trace of the nervous fear she'd always exuded in Simon's presence. He, on the other hand, seemed quiet, introspective, a far cry from the brusque, arrogant 'Señor' who ruled his home and family with unyielding, unassailable domination. When he turned to greet us, there was a sadness, almost a look of humility on the strong, craggy face.

'So you're leaving us,' Simon said. There was no accusatory or angry tone to his voice. Rather, a kind of resigned regret.

'Yes, sir,' Roger answered. 'It seems best. But we won't be far away. I'll be practicing in Los Angeles and I can be here in a very few minutes when . . . that is, *if* you need me.'

Natalie smiled. 'We know that, darling. And we'll send for you when . . . *if* we need you.' She reached for my hand. 'But it isn't just Roger we need. It's you, too, Virginia. You are our daughter. And we love you very much. We hope to see as much as we can of both of you . . . as often as we can, for as long as we can.'

I was choking back the tears and I saw Roger swallow hard. Natalie looked distressed. 'Oh, please, don't be upset! I'm happier than I've ever been in so many, many years. Perhaps happier than I've ever been in my whole life. I didn't want to keep my illness from all of you, but Simon thought it best. He was afraid that you'd not be able to act naturally around me and that I'd be more worried for you than for myself. But I knew you'd all do what I hoped – go on with your own lives, as you have, as you should. I'm really glad Carmelita made a mistake with the medication. It indirectly brought out so many things that should have been aired years ago. I feel so peaceful now. So relieved that all my children have a chance at happiness before it's too late. And,' she looked lovingly at Simon, 'that my dearest husband no longer needs to fear any disruption in life here that might disturb me.'

Simon cleared his throat. His words did not come easily.

'I'm sorry I made things hard for you, Virginia. I didn't know so many things.' His voice trembled. 'God forgive me for what I did. Not just to you. To both my sons and my daughter. And to Dolores.' He bit his lip. 'Pride. It's a terrible thing. The worst sin of all.'

Natalie reached out her hand to him. 'My dear, you mustn't,' she said. 'You *were* wrong about Dolores and André. Yes, that was a sin of pride. But you didn't know about Lila. None of us did. You didn't deliberately withhold help from her. You could never do such a thing, Simon. Never.'

I groped for the right words. 'It's easy to misunderstand, Mr. Trippe. I misunderstood you. And you me. I'm only happy that the truth is finally out. And in time for all of us.'

'Thank you,' Simon Trippe said, 'but there's one other thing I want you to know. It's about that day at the stables. The day of the fire. I wouldn't let Josh go into the woods and I tried to stop you because I knew that Lila wasn't there. You see, Drew told me he had seen her running down the road to her own house. I had no cause to doubt him.'

'I know that's true,' I said. 'Just as you and Dolores had no cause to doubt Lila's doctors. Even though in their case it was a human error and not a deliberate lie.'

Simon nodded. 'You're a fine girl. Roger is almost as fortunate as I've been.' He turned to my husband and clasped his hand. 'Take care of your wife, son. And take care of yourself.'

Abruptly, as though he was ashamed of his sentiment, Simon Trippe rushed out of the room. Natalie looked after him, a world of love in her eyes.

'Bless you both,' she said. 'Now be on your way. And don't worry. André will look after me medically. But it's Simon who will give me strength.'

She kissed us gently and slowly made her way

upstairs. Mrs. Angus saw us out.

'They're good people,' she said. 'I think you know that now. I've known it always.'

The door closed softly behind us. As we started down the driveway I looked back at the big house. Natalie Trippe was silhouetted in the window of her bedroom. Gracefully she raised a hand to her lips. Then she blew us a delicate kiss that was at once a farewell and a benediction.

THE RICH AND THE RIGHTEOUS

by Helen Van Slyke

Joseph Haylow, the dynamic, well-meaning founder of a billion-dollar empire, faces his testimonial retirement dinner with trepidation. Unwilling to retire from the company that is his creation, he must name his successor, a decision still unresolved as the dinner begins. Haylow's world, faith and family are examined as, in his last year of office, he learns the truth about those who surround him – the weak, the ruthless, the loving and the fallible.

THE HEART LISTENS

by Helen Van Slyke

THE HEART LISTENS is the story of Elizabeth Quigly, a woman of infinite compassion and courage who fails, if at all, only because she is ready to give too much.

In loving detail *THE HEART LISTENS* follows Elizabeth through her long and richly varied life, intimately describing her relationships, her joys, disappointments, and her incredible capacity to survive misfortune – and not only to survive, but to retain optimism and go forward to new and wonderful achievements.

With rare skill the author has sensitively explored many facets of love – though this book is much more than a recital of love affairs. *THE HEART LISTENS* has at its centre a strong, memorable woman. Elizabeth Quigly will catch your imagination as you begin the book, and will have won your sympathy and affection long before you reach its end.

NEW ENGLISH LIBRARY